CONTINUUM 4

Also Edited by Roger Elwood

CONTINUUM 4

Edited by Roger Elwood

A BERKLEY MEDALLION BOOK
published by
BERKLEY PUBLISHING CORPORATION

Berkley Publishing Corporation
200 Madison Avenue
New York, N. Y. 10016

Library of Congress Catalog Card Number: 73-87184

SBN 425-03077-6

*BERKLEY MEDALLION BOOKS are published by
Berkley Publishing Corporation
200 Madison Avenue
New York, N.Y. 10016*

BERKLEY MEDALLION BOOK ® TM 757,375

Printed in the United States of America

Berkley Medallion Edition, MARCH, 1976

Contents

Philip José Farmer

STATIONS OF THE NIGHTMARE

CHAPTER FOUR

Part 4. Passing On

[1.]

WINDLIKE, ghostlike, he raced around the earth.

When he was human, Earth was solid and horizon-bound. When he was saucer, it was a complex pattern of shifting triangles and cubes. Land was dully glowing chestnut and silver. Water was brightly glowing scarlet and gold. The three-cornered shapes and hollow cubes of land were smaller than those of water. The Gulf Stream was the same color as the rest of the Atlantic, but the cubes orbited more closely around the triangles.

Clouds of water were toadstools. Smog was a herd of shapes like porcupine fish. The clear air, of which there was very little, was like the snow on the screen of a malfunctioning TV set. Rain and snow alike were polyhedrons, but rain was azure and snow was burnt orange.

That was as "seen" from the stratosphere. When he raced close to the earth, the triangles and cubes merged, became still, became shades of green. The trees were upside-down

1

pyramids, looking more like strangely shaped tumors of the earth than separate entities.

At times he slowed down and eased up to a house. He "looked" into the windows. Dogs resembled astrakhans; cats, gas jets; humans, the symbols on the dollar bill, pyramids with one great crimson eye, always expanding or shrinking.

Around and around, up and down. And nowhere another of his kind. He should have accepted the invitation of his "mother," and thus he could have journeyed through space to the planet of some far-off star with her as a companion and guide. Now, if he lived a thousand years, and he would, he might never see another of his own. On the other hand (only a figure of speech, since he had no hands in this form), he might run into a dozen the day after tomorrow. The night after tomorrow, rather, since he flew only late at night. In the daytime of the United States of America, he walked on two legs.

He did not need sleep. To metamorphose was to lose the need for sleep. Something happened in his altered body which did away with the toxics accumulated as biped. The poisons streamed out behind as he soared, dark green, flattened spheres mixed with the sapphire quills that traced the change of angle in his flight.

A falling star, he shot toward his apartment, braked with a flare of white-edged blue comets, stopped before the open window, and entered. The transition was so quick that any human eye would have seen only a blur. And he was in the form which billions knew as Paul Eyre.

[2.]

Being human had its advantages. When he sped like a saucer-shaped Santa Claus from pole to pole, he browsed on photons, gravitons, X rays, magnetic lines, and chronotrons. But they were tasteless. Not so the buttered toast, the crisp bacon, the fried egg, the cantaloupe, the coffee. Intake was delicious, and so was output. Before the change, he had excreted with haste and shame, though he had been too dull to know that was the situation. Now he experienced a near ecstasy; getting rid of was not the same as taking in, but it was just as pleasurable. He shaved, showered, and dressed, read for four hours and, at seven-thirty, walked out of his apartment. The day manager and the guards said hello and looked at him with a barely concealed dislike, fear, and awe. Ostensibly, they were there to protect him. Actually, they were protecting the others from him. The others were the rest of humanity.

Practically, they were incapable of protecting him or the others.

He walked out of the building. Across the street was another apartment building. It held rooms in which many dozens of people, around the clock, trained cameras or listened to wire taps or swiveled directional microphones. He had "seen" them at night, their pulsing eyes glowing. They were reporting to various agencies in Washington, in Europe, and in Asia. They spied on him and on each other.

He walked swiftly twelve blocks and turned into a driveway leading to a huge old mansion. Once it had belonged to a rich family, then it had been a funeral home, and now it was his headquarters. The crowd along the driveway and on the porch cheered as he walked among them. They reached out their hands, though they never touched him. He made a gesture that they should draw back, and they surged like a wave withdrawing from a beach. They loved him, and they hated him.

Of the thousand or so on the parking lot, the grounds, the sidewalk, and the porch, half were the lame, the halt, the blind, the dying. The others were relatives or friends or the hired, bringing those on crutches, stretchers, and wheelchairs. He could, and would, send most of the sick home with their diseases left behind as abandoned baggage. But what could he do for the others, those defined as healthy? What could he do for greed, hate, prejudice, and self-loathing?

Lepers all.

He stopped on the porch, turned around, and held up his hand. Silence floated. "Go home now!" he said. "Make way for the others!"

3

There were cries of joy and amazement. Crutches soared. Men and women danced and cried. Children stood up from wheelchairs. Some, still on stretchers, were rushed to waiting ambulances. They were the ones whose convalescence would take some time. A woman whose misshapen bones were beginning to jell cried out in fear. But she would be all right in a few weeks.

A man near the foot of the steps to the porch suddenly reached into his coat pocket and brought out a revolver. His face was pale and contorted.

"Die, you filthy anti-Christ!" he screamed. "Die and go to hell!"

Hate was snatched away by pain. He dropped the revolver and clutched at his chest. Two plaincothesmen moved toward him, but they were too late. He was dead on the sidewalk by the time they had reached him.

Paul Eyre murmured, "They never learn!"

[3.]

In the beginning, he had sat in a large office while the "patients" walked by or were carried before him. They had entered one door and without pausing or speaking proceeded to the exit. There was no business to transact except that of getting people in and out as swiftly as possible. Each was handed a card which stated that if the recipient cared to, he could send whatever sum he felt like sending to this address. Paul Eyre did not doubt that among his employees were agents of the American Medical Association and the Food and Drug Administration. They watched him as if he were a hawk among chickens and he owner of the chickens. But their reports were monotonous, unspiced by irregularities.

After a few months, Eyre had moved out onto the porch. In warm weather, he looked at the passersby through screens. In cold weather, the porch was glassed in. Automobiles, trucks, and buses crept by on the horse-shaped driveway and the street while he looked at the pale and hopeful faces in them.

To heal, he had to see them in the flesh, though a single glance sufficed.

On the other hand, he did not have to see to kill. Snipers hidden in rooms many stories above him fell dead as they put their finger on the trigger. An automatic device set to gas him, operating by a time clock so there would be no direct human initiation, had gone up in smoke. A suicidal fanatic had tried to fly his nitroglycerine-loaded airplane into his headquarters, but it had blown up while over the Illinois River. A time bomb had exploded in the face of a man before he could get it into his car.

There had doubtless been many other fatal incidents about which Paul Eyre knew nothing.

That was, to him, the strange thing about his powers. He had not the slightest idea how they operated. There was no tickling, no tingling, no change in body temperature, no outward or inward manifestation of energy transmitted or withdrawn.

He had established, however, that he did not kill just because he disliked or hated a person. The power was activated only when a person was about to be an immediate physical danger to him.

He was an enigma for more than himself. Everybody, even the Indian in the remote Amazon jungle or the aborigine in the great Australian desert, had heard of him. They came from everywhere, and business in Busiris, Illinois, boomed. Every motel, hotel, and rooming house was jammed. Motels and restaurants were going up like telephone poles. The police department had had to double its traffic division, but there were no outcries from the taxpayers. Eyre was paying for the new personnel. There were protests from Eyre's neighbors about the crowded streets, but nobody could do anything about this. And "the Eyrecraft industry," as the local paper termed it, had brought prosperity to Busiris. It was the largest industry in the county, larger even than the giant Trackless Diesel Motor Corporation for which Eyre had once worked.

And so he sat on the porch, even during his lunch period, or paced back and forth while the sick were carried by. At seven in the evening, he walked off the porch. His staff would stay for another two or three hours to complete their work. But he was through for the day; ten hours and thirty-odd thousand people were enough for him. Too much. He was exhausted though he had done nothing except sit, walk, and confer with his manager and secretaries occasionally. He walked home without a bodyguard, though the sidewalks and streets would be crowded with the sick, waiting for him to see them.

He dined alone in his apartment except for the three evenings a week that his current mistresses visited him. These were beautiful young women who had their peculiar reasons for wanting to bed with him. Some were grateful because he had healed them or relatives or husbands. Some felt they adored him because he was a miracle worker. Some, he found out later, were agents for the AMA, the IRS, the FBI, Russia, China, Cuba, England, Israel, the United Arab Republic, Germany (West and East), and India. Some had even asked him to take refuge in their countries. Their countries had tried to kidnap him, with fatal results for the agents, so now they were trying to seduce him. He never turned them over to the FBI (in one case, the young woman was working for both Albania and the FBI). He merely told them to leave and quit bothering him.

Sometimes, he would go to the window and look down at the street. It was white with faces turned up to him as if he were the sun and they the plants. Their murmur came up to him even through the soundproofing. "Heal me," it cried, "and I will be happy!"

He knew better, but he healed them anyway. He couldn't help himself.

Somebody had once suggested that he fly over the world while the sick were brought out into the open spaces for him to look down upon. He had rejected this. Even if he could cover every square foot of the planet in a single day, he would have a million new patients the next day. But to travel by plane around and around the globe would be to lose all his privacy. How could he leave his quarters at night and girdle the earth, search the skies, sublunary space, Africa, Polynesia, and the South Pole? No, here at least, he had made

6

arrangements to leave by the back window which faced a court where no one could come. No doubt, it was under electronic and photographic surveillance. But his watchers were government officials, and their reports were top secret. They didn't believe what they reported. Some things are so impossible that to admit you believe them is to admit that you're crazy. Between the two was a credibility fuse easily blown in human beings.

Why had Paul Eyre become the great healer? Why had he subjected himself to a boring duty which could never achieve its goal, the extermination of all physical diseases in mankind? For one thing, he didn't have the heart to turn the sick away. For another, he was getting rich, and he needed much money to pay for the support of his daughter and his ex-wife. And, last but by no means least, he was, being human when in human form, gratified by the attention and the idolization. He was the most important man on the planet. Important in a way which the public did not even suspect. If they had, they would have tried to tear him apart, literally. He shuddered when he thought of it, not because the mob would succeed, because they wouldn't. It was the vision of hundreds, perhaps thousands, dropping dead at the same time that sickened him. So far, the few known deaths, his would-be murderers, had been explained away as caused by excitement combined with a weak heart. Though none of his attackers had had heart trouble, fake medical histories had been supplied. The pathologists who did the dissections did not have to be bribed to validate these. They always found the heart ruptured, even when it looked healthy.

Eyre read for a while after eating the meal ordered from a delicatessen. (No need to test it; the poisoner would have died before he could touch the food.) He put the book aside and watched TV for half an hour, then turned it off. How trivial even his favorite programs seemed. Bullshit and nonsense, as his friend, Tincrowdor, was fond of saying.

Tincrowdor. Was he a friend? When Eyre had been held in prison, Tincrowder had helped him. At the same time, Tincrowdor had thought of ways to kill him. But that, Tincrowdor had explained, had been done because he did not really believe that Eyre could be killed. Besides, the intellectual challange had been too much for him. He had to try.

He went to the phone and called the switchboard downstairs. He waited, while the ringing went on and on. How many were listening in? At least a dozen American government agencies, the AMA, and half a dozen foreign agents. Trolls eavesdropping on the troll killer. Helpless to do anything but listen and then make their reports.

At last, a boozy male voice answered. "Leo Queequeg Tincrowdor, poet laureate of B-T-A-O-C, speaking."

If the unwary caller asked what the letters meant, Tincrowdor would reply, "Busiris, the asshole of creation."

"Come on over," Eyre said. "I'd like to talk to you."

"You're not mad at me?"

"I just want to talk. That is, if you're fairly sober."

"I'm fairly," Tincrowdor said. "Tell your gorillas not to shoot."

"They're just here to watch me," Eyre said, "not to protect me. You could come in with a bazooka, and they'd only ask you to produce your ID." Which was not much of an exaggeration.

[4.]

Before Tincrowdor arrived, another visitor phoned from the lobby. This was Dr. Lehnhausen, the righthand man of the President of the United States. Eyre was surprised, though not very much. Lehnhausen had made unannounced trips before, flying in secretly from Washington, talking to him for an hour or so, and then departing as swiftly as he had come.

A minute later, Eyre admitted Lehnhausen. Four men stood guard, two by the door, one at the elevator, and one at the end of the hall, near the fire escape.

Lehnhausen was a tall, dark man with a slight German accent. He waved his hand at Eyre and said, "How are you, sir?"

"I'm never sick, and I'm always busy," Eyre said. "And you?"

"That depends upon what you tell me," Lehnhausen said. "I'm here to ask you to reconsider your decision. *He* told me that he hoped you would remember that you are an American."

How I would have thrilled at those words only a year ago! Eyre thought. The President himself asking me to do my duty, to defend my country.

"I never said no," Eyre said. "I thought I'd made that clear. What I did say, and you were there and know it, is that it's not necessary for me to live in Washington or to be advised by a bunch of generals and bureaucrats. I will defend this nation, but it will be done automatically. And it doesn't matter where I am."

"Yes, we understand that," Lehnhausen said. "But what if the President believes that it is necessary to launch an atomic missile attack before another nation does?"

"I don't know," Eyre said. He began to pace back and forth and to sweat. "I have tried repeatedly to explain that I have no control over this, this power. Anything that is an immediate threat to me seems to be killed. An atomic war would threaten me, even if the attack were launched from this country at another one. The enemy would retaliate, of course, and that would be a threat. To stop this, I, or whatever is working inside me, might decide that the man who gives the word to attack should drop dead before he can give that word.

"This means that whoever starts to give the word, to press the button, would die. Which means that there is no need for the President to order an attack. The attack he would be trying to forestall would never come. The enemy executive would die before he could give the order. The man succeeding him would die, and so on.

"So, there is no call for the President to give his order. Do you see what I mean? God knows I've told you enough times, and I find this visit unnecessary and annoying. I can't seem to get the truth through to you people in Washington."

Lehnhausen said, bitterly, "What you have done is to nullify our atomic potential. We can't use it, and that places us at a disadvantage with nations which have a greater potential in conventional means of warfare. Both the Soviet Union and China can assemble far larger armies than we can. The Soviet Union's navy is larger than ours. Russia could take over Europe at any time, and there is nothing we could do about it. And China could take over Asia. Then what would happen?''

"I don't know," Eyre said. "Perhaps I—this thing in me, rather—might decide that an invasion of the Old World by these two powers would be an immediate threat to me. It might kill the Chinese or Russian leaders before they could give the order to attack. I don't know. I do know that it would probably decide that an invasion of this country by any power would be an immediate threat. In which case, there wouldn't be any invasion.''

"But there might be one of the Old World, and you'd do nothing," Lehnhausen said.

"You make me sound like a traitor," Eyre said. "Can't I convince you that I have absolutely no control? Anyway, you have told me that the foreign governments have found out all this, and they won't attack because they're afraid that their executives would drop dead if they did order one. Not that they are going to. All this is hypothetical.''

Lehnhausen said, "You were a minuteman once. You resigned when the organization was declared an illegal one. I would think. . . .''

"I'm not the Paul Eyre of that time.''

"Sometimes we wonder if you're Paul Eyre at all," Lehnhausen said.

Eyre laughed. He knew what Lehnhausen was thinking. Tincrowdor had explained to him that some of the higher-ups had to be convinced that he could change into a thing that was alien to the Earth. And some of them would then conclude that the real Paul Eyre had been killed and his place taken by this thing. This thing, this creature, "this monster from outer space," had come to take over the Earth or, at least, to wreck it so that it would be helpless before the invasion that would follow.

"Science fiction stories and horror movies have conditioned people to think along these lines," Tincrowdor said. "I've thought the same thing myself, but I've observed you closely. You're the original Paul Eyre all right. At least, half the original. You may be possessed, but you're not wholly possessed."

For the first time, Paul Eyre fully realized that he was the only free man on the planet. He could do anything he wished and nobody could stop him. He could move to any country he wished, and the authorities could not stop him. Neither the U.S. nor the country in which he wished to live could do a thing. He could live where he chose, steal, rob openly, rape, and murder, and he would be unhindered.

He had no wish to do any of this, which was fortunate. But what if somebody else had had his experience? What if some immoral man had encountered that creature in the woods near that farm?

And what kind of a world would it be if everybody had his powers? Nobody would dare to threaten anybody else. But what about a quarrel in which both thought they were right? This was the usual situation. Would both arguers die? Not unless each intended physical harm to the other. Which meant that the violent one would be the one to die.

"There's nothing to talk about," Eyre said. "I'm getting tired of being bugged by you and the other government officials."

That includes the President, he thought. But he could not bring himself to say it. He still had some awe of the chief executive.

"I don't want to see you again, or hear from you any more, unless it's a national emergency. And I doubt that there's any need for that even then. The emergency will be over before you're aware of it."

"You're not God!" Lehnhausen said. "Even though there are some fanatics who claim you are!"

"I've publicly rejected those nuts," Eyre said. "It's not my fault that they pay no attention to what I say."

He looked at his wristwatch. "I have an appointment. So why don't you go now?"

"You're just a citizen. . . !" Lehnhausen said and stopped. The eyes behind the thick glasses were bulging, and his face was red.

He swallowed, took out a handkerchief, wiped his glasses and his forehead, put the glasses back on, and tried to smile. He held the handkerchief in a tight fist.

"You're safe unless you try to use violence," Eyre said softly.

"I had no such intention," Lehnhausen said. "Very well. If you won't do your duty. . . ."

"Can't, not won't."

"The result is the same. But, as I started to say, the President would like at least one assurance from you. The election will take place in a year, and. . . ."

"And you want my promise that I won't run for president," Eyre said. "But I told him that I had no such ambitions."

"People have been known to change their minds."

"I'm neither qualified nor interested. I'd make a mess of things. There was a time when I was ignorant enough to believe that I could do better than anybody else in the White House. But my horizons have broadened since then. I'm still ignorant, but not that ignorant."

"We know that you've been approached by the Democrats, the Socialist Labor Party, the Communists, and the Messianists. If you. . . ."

"If I did run, it'd be as a Republican," Eyre said. "And the first thing I'd do would be to get rid of those people who are trying to kill me. You'd be among them."

Lehnhausen turned pale, and he said, "I deny that!"

"I suspect that the man who tried to kill me this morning was one of your agents. That anti-Christ business was just to make people think he was a religious fanatic."

"You're getting paranoiac," Lehnhausen said.

"A paranoiac is one who has no rational basis for suspecting persecution. I know that you've been trying to assassinate me."

"Assassination implies a political motive," Lehnhausen said. "The correct word is murder."

"You have a political motive," Eyre said. "But it's not the main motive. Good-bye, Mr. Lehnhausen."

Lehnhausen hesitated and then, slowly, pulled a paper from his coat pocket. "Would you sign a statement that you will not be a candidate?"

"No," Eyre said. "My word is good enough. Good-bye."

[5.]

"That's the first time you ever asked me about my middle name," Tincrowdor said. "Hadn't curiosity ever entered that dull mind of yours before?"

"I always thought it was an Indian name and that you had Indian blood and didn't want to admit it," Eyre said.

"I do have Miami Indian ancestors," Tincrowdor said. "But I'm not the least bit ashamed of it. Queequeg, however, is supposed to be a Polynesian name, though it certainly doesn't have that melodious vowel-filled substance which distinguishes all Polynesian words. I think Melville made it up. In any event, my father read a lot, even if he was an electrical engineer. His favorite book was *Moby Dick*, and his favorite character was the giant harpooner, Queequeg. So he named me after the son of the king of the island of Kokovoko. *It is not down in any map; true places never are.* So says Ishmael.

"If I'd been given any choice in the business, I would have taken Tashtego as my name. That Indian stuck to his job to the last, nailing up the defiant flag of Ahab even as the Pequod sank, and catching the wing of the sky hawk between the spar and his hammer, taking a living bit of heaven with him down to hell. A fine bit of symbolism, though rather too obvious for anybody for Melville to get away with it.

"On the other hand, my father probably knew what he was doing when he labeled my character before it was formed. Queequeg thought much about his death, and so do I. Queequeg prepared his coffin while he was still living, and so do I. His was stiff wood and carved with many strange symbols.

13

Mine is fluid alcohol, and the carving is done with the bending of the elbow. Both of us float alive in our coffins."

Tincrowdor poured himself another drink, sniffed at it, and said, "Zounds! This is the best the world, and Kentucky, offers."

"Let's get back to the subject," Eyre said.

"The only true subject is oneself, and I never get off it. So where were we?"

"Extrapolating. And I wish you'd quit drinking. You said your memory and your creativity have been much better since you started seeing me. Your drinking had caused brain damage, and I had reversed the irreversible. Yet you continue to destroy your brain."

"Why not, as long as I can still be healed by coming into your holy presence? When you go forever, I'll quit. Or try to."

"And you think I'll go?"

"I would advise you to leave now. I don't mean tomorrow morning. I mean right now. You're staying for only two reasons, neither of which should be considered. One, you can't shuck off guilt because you'll be deserting your family, which you have done, anyway, and the sick people of this earth. Forget them. They're going to die anyway, and you can never cure all of them or anything but a small portion. Earth breeds sick humans faster than a dozen Paul Eyres could heal them. Second, you could stay here a thousand years and no mate would come. So get out to the stars and look for one."

Tincrowdor swallowed three ounces, smacked his lips, and said, "I forgot. There are two other reasons. Third, let humanity go its own way. Let it choose its own destiny, miserable as that probably will be. Man was not meant to be a flying saucer. Fourth, if you hang around this planet, you will inevitably be killed."

Eyre started a little and said, "How could they do that?"

"I don't know, but they'll figure out a way. Man's stupidity is only exceeded by his ingenuity. You're a challenge to our survival, and think tanks all over the world are working three shifts a day contriving means for your destruction.

Somebody is going to come up with the solution, and you'll be dissolved.''

"I don't see how."

"You've been given godlike powers, but your imagination hasn't been improved much. *Of course*, you can't see."

"Can you?"

"Don't look at me so narrow-eyed. I'm no danger to you. Not now. I quit thinking up ways. At least, I'm not telling anybody about them."

"All right," Eyre said. "I am sick of this never-ending task. It's no joy to go to bed knowing that thousands more are waiting in motel rooms to see me in the morning, that thousands more are traveling to see me the morning after. Yet, I feel that the poor devils need me, and my conscience would hurt me if I abandoned them.

"But I also feel that I am neglecting my main duty. I should be out there, looking for someone with whom I can be a true mate. Someone, or something, with whom I can share an ecstasy that you . . . . human beings, I mean . . . can never know."

"One is a duty; the other is a joy. That's what you mean," Tincrowdor said.

"And my manifest duty," Eyre said.

"You talk as if you're a nation, not a person," Tincrowdor said.

"I could bear nations within me."

"Yes, you *could*," Tincrowdor said, looking as if surprise had sobered him. "You could carry millions of saucer-gametes within you. Fly over a populated city, release the yellow cloud, and hundreds, maybe thousands, would become impregnated or spermified, or however you want to put it. And that would mean the end of the human race. As we know it, anyway."

"That is what I don't understand," Eyre said. "For the sake of efficiency, the gametes should be distributed among a dense population. Why was the yellow cloud released when I was the only one who could be affected?"

"We have to assume, for logical reasons, that it was an accident. You fired at what you thought was a quail, but it

15

was the, uh, saucerperson. Your shotgun pellets wounded her and brought forth the gametes before their time.''

"Yes, but why didn't I drop dead before I fired? And what about her wounds? When I saw her later, in her other form, she didn't have a scar."

"The latter first. She, and I suppose you, have wonderful self-healing properties. If you can heal others, why not your-self? As for her vulnerability, perhaps the saucer form doesn't have the killing powers that the human form has. The gamete that fused with you has the power to protect itself while it's in a fragile form, that is, yours. The adult form, or at least the saucer form, doesn't have this. Why, I don't know, since you have it when you revert to the human form.''

Tincrowdor took another drink and then said, "But perhaps you're not an adult yet. Or perhaps the adult just doesn't have the ability to kill by thought, or however it's done. Remember, when she fled the prison yard with machine gun bullets flying around her, the guards shooting at her didn't drop dead. I find that significant.''

Eyre tried to keep the alarm out of his voice.

"Then why haven't they tried to kill me when I'm in that . . . saucer . . . form? They must be watching my window. They've seen me shoot in and out of it and they've tracked me with radar. I know that, because I've fed on the radar waves.''

"What happened? Their instruments were missing every other wave? They didn't get a complete echo? ''

"I don't know. But they must have thought something was wrong with their equipment.''

Tincrowdor laughed. He said. "They didn't shoot at you because it never occurred to them that you might be lacking your powers when in that metamorph.''

"Then nobody knows?''

Tincrowdor hesitated and said, "I know. At least, I sus-pect.''

"And you've told nobody?''

"Nobody.''

Eyre was not worried that their conversation was being monitored. He didn't care that the phones were tapped, but he

16

could not endure being overheard when he was talking to the women who visited him. Two men came in twice a day and swept the apartment for electronic bugs, and he himself checked it out in the evening with equipment supplied by the FBI.

"Cross your heart and hope to die?" Eyre said, grinning.

"I'm afraid that I *would* die," Tincrowdor said.

[6.]

While racing as a tiny satellite of the earth and while sitting or walking in his apartment, Eyre had tried to communicate with the entity in his brain. Silence was the only response. Silence and emptiness. He did not feel that he was occupied. He was alone. Singular.

Yet he knew about the tests which the now dead Dr. Croker had made. The first of these had revealed that his blood and other tissues were swarming with microscopic creatures. They looked more like yellow bricks with rounded edges than anything. Then these were gone, presumably excreted, except for one, which had been located in his brain.

It was this organism which had given him his powers to kill, to cure, and to metamorphose. This, according to Tincrowdor, was a sort of gamete, analogous to a human ovum. Eyre, though composed of trillions of cells, was another gamete, the sperm. The saucer-gamete had fused with him to make a new individual. The fusing was not, however, necessarily physical. It could be solely psychical. Or it could be psychosomatic.

Whatever its final stage in him, it seemed to carry ancestral memories, and it seemed to communicate these to Eyre through dreams. Time and again, while sleeping, he had visions of a glimmering green city, many-domed, many-towered, far away beyond fields of red flowers. Sometimes he had seen creatures that looked like leocentaurs, half human, half lion. Sometimes, he was a female leocentaur and he, or she, mated. Sometimes, he was in saucer form and

17

voyaging between stars, pulling himself along on the crumpled fabric of space and eating light and other forms of energy.

In the past six months, these dreams had ceased. Did that mean that the entity was no longer separate but had fused with him? And if it had, why did he, Eyre, feel unchanged, totally human? That is, he did when he was in bipedal form. When in saucer form, he felt almost all nonhuman, though if someone had been able to ask him his name, he would have replied that it was Paul Eyre.

Tincrowdor had said that it was not true that Eyre was unchanged. He had a perceptiveness and a compassion he had lacked before. But that could be due to the shock of the events he had experienced. These had shaken loose qualities which had always existed in him but which, for some reason probably grounded in his childhood, he had suppressed.

"Possibly," Tincrowdor had said, "the entity is dominant when the saucer form is used. It takes over your brain then, though the possession is so subtle that you think you are in control. When in human form, you are dominant, though it is evident that the entity still uses its survival powers. However, these may be potentialities which have always existed in the human psychosoma but which only a very few have been aware of or have been able to use. Examples: so-called witch doctors or medicine men in so-called primitive societies.

"It is possible, as I've said, that these powers exist only when you're in human form. When in saucer form, you rely on speed to survive. The only way to find out is to make a test. And you can't do that, because if you're powerless, then you'll be killed. Knowledge, in this case, would not be worth the price."

This was the dilemma which occupied much of his human time. When hurtling through air or just above it, when racing across the fields or skimming cities, he did not think of it. He felt too much joy to let terrestrial concerns into his consciousness. The joy was, it was true, tempered by a dull sadness on not finding a mate. But this intrusion took place only when dawn threatened the mid-west and he returned home.

Tonight, after Tincrowdor had left, he sped out of the

18

window and soared vertically upward. For the first time, he determined to leave the sublunary space and to visit the moon itself. Perhaps there might be one of his kind there, though something told him that the chances were not high. It was an easy and swift journey; he was not handicapped by complex problems of orbital computation and power expenditure. All he had to do was point himself at the moon, overtake it, match his velocity with its, increase or decrease his velocity, and circle around and around it, swoop down, nestle for a while, soar up again, and streak for earth. The whole trip, according to the clock in his apartment, had taken three hours and four and a half minutes. An hour of that had been spent exploring the moon's surface.

The following Saturday and Sunday, he visited Mars and its two moons, Deimos and Phobos.

The weekend after that, he visited Venus, but he did not stay long in its heavy, cloud-laden atmosphere. As he shot through it, battling against titanic winds and tiny particles whose nature he did not know, he detected something living far, far down. It was shadowy huge, vaguely spindle-shaped, and it radiated danger. He curved upward in a burst of speed which brought him near the burning point. His panic did not subside until he had put himself far above the atmosphere. When he had regained his apartment and his human form, he wept and sobbed. Whatever his own powers were, he would have been caught like a mouse by a cat and destroyed in some horrible manner if he had not reacted so swiftly. That thing would have ingested him but would not have killed all of him. A piece of him would have suffered hell for eons before his last spark had fallen into darkness.

He rarely needed sleep, but this morning he was squeezed with fatigue. He lay down on the bed without putting on his pajamas and slept, though not well. Twice he woke up moaning with horror as something black and shapeless tried to pull him into itself.

The horror weighed him during the days and nights that followed. For the first time, he did not feel safe when in saucer form. If such a thing could exist on Venus, what might he find on Jupiter or Pluto?

One Saturday morning he made up his mind. He would leave Earth and the human race and go seek another of his kind. He needed the companionship they could provide, though he had no idea of what its nature would be. Whatever it was, it surely must be superior to that which men and women had given him. Or, to be fair, that which he had given them. Something in him had made him a loner, no matter how gregarious he might seem to others. He had had no true friends, people with whom he felt comfortable and intimate. His efforts at conversation had been ludicrous and boring. He felt at ease only around machines, which explained why they had taken so much of his time or why he had given them so much time. He could handle them, could analyze their malfunctions and repair them. But his acquaintances, his fellow workers, his family were enigmas. He was out of phase with them, and the one with whom he had been most intimate was a stranger whom he hated and who hated him. If he had had his present perceptiveness when he had married Mavice, he could have saved the marriage and even been happy with it. But it was too late for that now.

Maybe his meeting the saucer-sphinx thing in the woods had not been an accident. Maybe it, she, rather, had sensed that he could make the transition to nonhuman form easier than most humans she had surveyed. His roots were shallow and in loose soil; being torn from humanity would not be difficult or too painful for him.

There were too many maybes. He wanted certainty and knowledge, and the only way for him to gain these was to venture out after those who could give him facts.

And so, having decided, he picked up the Sunday morning paper and saw that which changed his mind again.

[7.]

He read the story on page two of the A section and then phoned downstairs for Chicago and St. Louis papers. These had the same story but in more detail than the local journal.

FLYING SAUCER SEEN IN LOS ALAMOS AREA
UFO LANDS IN NEW MEXICO
RADAR AND EYEWITNESSES SEE VISITOR FROM SPACE?

"Yesterday, April 1 (April Fool's Day), at 5:32 P.M., MST, a busload of government workers saw. . . ."

". . . radar detected and held on its screen for two minutes a UFO. . . ."

". . . the pilot reports seeing the object land on top of a hill. . . ."

". . . officials refuse to make any comment. . . ."

Eyre read everything about the "conventionally shaped UFO" and then turned on the TV. Not until the five o'clock news was there any mention of the UFO, and that was a brief comment by a broadcaster who obviously thought it was a hoax. But there was a photograph of a blurred object supposedly taken by a guard near the test area. This had been the scene of a number of hydrogen bomb experiments in the late 1960's.

Eyre thought several times about leaving at once, even though it was daylight. What difference did it make now if he broke his vow to himself not to change shape until the sun had long been down? He probably wouldn't be coming back, and so what did he care that passersby might see him? Let them talk. The story wouldn't increase the amount of attention on him, anyway.

But he did not follow his impulse. He might not find her (why did he think of it as her when it might be another male?). If she were gone, had come to Earth for only a little while, he would have to go after her. But he might not find her. He had no way of determining toward what sector of space she would be flying.

However, it did not seem likely that she would stay for only a little while. She might be ready to "give birth" to a cloud of gametes and so was looking for a concentration of humans. But if this were so, why had she picked out the remote and sparsely populated Los Alamos atomic testing grounds? Had she been attracted by some residue of radiation?

As soon as night came, he would go. The skies were starting to cloud and rain was predicted. It would be dark enough for him to leave then; he would go so fast that the human eye would not recognize him as anything but a streak. The human mind would classify him as an illusion, a temporary aberration of the eye. What did it matter what they thought?

A few minutes before the sun touched the horizon, he phoned Tincrowdor. "Hello, Leo. Paul. I'm going."

There was a pause, and then Tincrowdor, in a strange voice, said, "I thought you would. But listen, Paul, I. . . ."

"Never mind. Good-bye."

"But Paul. . . !"

Eyre hung up the phone and undressed. The phone began ringing. Tincrowdor was probably calling back, but he would have nothing to say that needed hearing. He would say that Eyre's first duty was to humanity (despite the many times he'd argued against that). He would remind Eyre that it was his presence that ensured against atomic war or even a large-scale conventional war. He would . . . what did it matter what he would say?

And so he slipped into his other form like a hand into a glove and flung the gauntlet of himself against the night.

[8.]

Around and around over what he thought was northern New Mexico, he sped. The earth was a shifting pattern of triangles and cubes, glowing brightly, varicolored, the hills blocks of silver nudging the chestnut triangles around them. And then far away, tiny, a light like that from a firefly's tail glowed. On, off. On, off. Dash, dot. Dash, dot. The longer pulses looked to him as if they were scarlet musical quarter notes written against an azure page so pale that he could see the vague geometrical forms of the earth behind it. The shorter pulses looked like six-branched candelabras enveloped in silver fuzz.

They gave him no shock of recognition. They were not what he had expected. Certainly, they were not radiations from his "mother," the creature that had passed him in space as she traveled toward some planet circling some far-off star. But then he had seen her moving, and the shape of his kind (his kind!) changed with velocity. No, it did not actually change, but his perception of her had changed as she changed vectors. This one must be resting on the ground.

She was, he thought excitedly, waiting for him.

But why here? Why hadn't she sought him out in his apartment?

Eyre could "see" in all directions and so perceived his downward angle of flight as double amphorae burning blue. Among them were little novae of green sputtering off into violet; these indicated that he was not just flying in a calm mood; he was thrilled with delight.

The pulses came faster, merged into expanding and disappearing obovoids and then became a many-rayed star with a yellow center. If he were in human form, he knew, he would see simply a saucer shape, light-gray, two feet in diameter, four inches high at the thickest part, the center. It would be lying in the middle of a plain over three miles wide; the wavering bands of purple would be cacti.

Or would it? A many-rayed star with a yellow center. There was something about that form and color that was familiar or at least should be familiar.

Where?

Suddenly, he knew.

He pulled up and away, but it was too late.

There was only one light, now, the blinding raving light of a sun. Or of atomic energy loosed, matter turning into energy, expanding.

Even as he raced away, its tongues lapping at him, he thought, How did they do it?

He had escaped being consumed, but he had not gone unhurt. The fireball had never enveloped him, but he had gone out of control for a while, turning over and over, falling, smashing into something, ricocheting high, regaining control, speeding, the air turning black around him, which meant that he was close to turning into fire himself from its friction.

And then the thing behind him had dropped away and was gone, and he was going home, mortally wounded.

No, he could not return to his apartment. There was no one there to ensure that his death would not be useless.

He would not be able to metamorphose into his human form again. That meant that he could not find out how they had tricked him. But there would be at least one human being who was going to inherit.

There might be more than one. He had passed over many towns and cities and lonely farmhouses on his erratic, sinking path homeward. Behind him, mixed with the double amphorae, was a trail of tiny but brightly golden nautilus-shell forms. When he was human, they would look like bricks. They were issuing from the ripped open shell of himself, and most of them had escaped before he became aware of them. Then he had squeezed down on something inside him and blocked off the little he had left. He was saving the residue.

Presently, as he thought he was out of strength and must fail, a hexagonal form loomed, and he was through it. It would be a window, the main one in Tincrowdor's bedroom. The sound of shattered glass and of a heavy object smashing into the floor, ramming into the wall, should bring Tincrowdor if he were home. He hoped he was home. Even if he were not, he would find Eyre here and would touch him, and there would be gametes all over the room and over himself.

The surface beneath him shivered with long flat waves of silver. The sound of approaching footsteps. Then, in the doorway, which was to him an iris, a figure appeared. It was pyramid-shaped with a great eyelike protuberance on top. Comets like those from a Fourth of July sparkler sprayed from the top of the eye. They would be the words of an excited man, and the man would be Tincrowdor. In the center of the eye was a dirigible shape, glowing green, the shape of human maleness. The dirigible bore in its center an X formed by two bottle shapes. How appropriate to Tincrowdor, he thought. No one else in the universe had that identifying shape.

"Good-bye, Tincrowdor," he thought. "Pass it on."

The shapes dissolved; the colors faded. Dimly, he could see the creature with the lion's lower body and the beautiful torso and head of a woman, and, even more dimly, the red fields and the green city. And then they, too, bleached out.

[10.]

The man said, "The President did not want to commend you by letter or phone. Why I don't know, so don't ask me. I was just told to deliver the message verbally."

Tincrowdor stood looking out of a window of the living room. The man sat on a sofa with a cup of coffee in one hand. Morna, Tincrowdor's wife, was not home. The man had made certain of that before he came to the house.

Out there in the moonless night was a field, and in the field was a towering and very old sycamore tree. Near its roots was a smooth place over which new grass was growing. Below the grass lay a hard shell ripped open at one end and within were decaying meat and worms. Only Tincrowdor knew that it was there because he had buried it, and he intended to tell no one about it. He did not want to repeat Eyre's history.

Was his blood swarming with millions of tiny yellow brick-shaped things? Probably. He had no intention of getting a doctor to examine his blood. This time, events would take a different course.

He turned and said, "So you don't know what the message means?"

The man looked alarmed. "If you try to tell me, I'll get up and walk out."

"No sweat," Tincrowdor said. "Well, you tell the President that mum is the word and that he doesn't have to worry about me. Not that he doesn't know that already. And tell him that I'm not sorry that he can't give me a medal. I wouldn't accept it. But you can tell him that if I'd known he was going to use my plan, I . . . well, anyway, tell him for me that he's a big liar. He promised. . . ."

The man looked bewildered. Tincrowdor said, "Never mind. Just tell him I said thanks for nothing."

The man put the cup down and rose. "Is that all?"

"That's all I have to say or ever will say on the subject. Which I'll bet you're dying to know. Which would be what *would* happen if you did know."

The man's eyebrows rose. He picked up his hat and said, "Good-bye, Mr. Tincrowdor." He did not offer to shake hands. But he hesitated at the doorway.

"Did you know Paul Eyre very well?"

"As well as anyone could."

"I'm asking because he cured my wife's terminal cancer, you know."

"I didn't know, but I can see why you can't restrain your curiosity."

"That *was* strange!" the man burst out. "Disappearing like that and no trace whatsoever! And guarded by two dozen men! FBI, too! Do you think that he just took off? Or did some foreign agents. . . ?"

"I wouldn't care to speculate."

"Well, at least the world will never be the same again."

Tincrowdor smiled and said, "You never spoke a truer word."

"A man like him never truly dies. He lives on in us."

"In some of us, anyway," Tincrowdor said. "Good-bye, Mr. Sands."

After the man had left, Tincrowdor poured himself another bourbon. Well, he thought, Eyre certainly knew whom he should revenge himself on. Came straight here. He couldn't have known, but he must have guessed that I originated the trap. But the president told me that the plan was rejected. And, later, I was glad that he had turned it down. I didn't really want to be responsible for Eyre's death.

When in the saucer form, the power to kill or cure by thought, or whatever, doesn't operate. So, catch Eyre in that form. And the bait? What he desired most, a mate. That rhymes, doesn't it?

Eyre told me how he perceived things, and so I knew he'd never be fooled by just a simulacrum. It would have to contain something living. And the shell did. It held a swarm of bees.

Eyre had been fooled long enough to get caught. The atomic bomb buried under the earth beneath the dummy had been triggered by a device connected to the radar. The image registered by the radar was the only one that would set the bomb off.

There were outcries from governments about illegal experimentation with bombs, even though the U.S. government had said that it was an accident. This was for public consumption. After the governmental heads had been informed, secretly, that Paul Eyre was dead, the objections were dropped, the excuses accepted.

Radar had tracked Eyre into the area of Busiris, Illinois, and he could imagine the consternation that must have caused. But when no remains were found, it had been concluded, or at least he supposed it had been, that Eyre had fallen into the river or somewhere in the woods around Busiris. A quiet search had been conducted without success. Months passed, and with these the jitters of the officials had evaporated.

There had been one thing which Tincrowdor had not understood. Eyre had had no mate, so how could he release a cloud of gametes? If the saucerperson released these, and there had been no cross-fertilization, then the gametes would contain only the genes of the mother.

After some wrestling with his mind, he had concluded that that did not matter. The being with whom a gamete fused would eventually find a mate. Or, if it did not, then it would pass on its gametes to another, who would in turn find a mate.

Or perhaps there was no mating, no cross-fertilization, not as terrestrial science defined it. Every adult form generated gametes in its body, and the purpose of these was to locate and fuse with a being of an entirely different genus. Maybe with a being of an entirely different kingdom, since the saucers might, for all he knew, be vegetables. Or some type of creature neither animal nor vegetable.

Whatever the theory, the reality proceeded unhindered.

He went to the window and lifted his glass in toast to the inert and invisible mass under the trees.

"You win, Paul Eyre. You and your kind. Soon to be my kind."

The door opened, and his wife, Morna, entered.

He said hello and kissed her, thinking as he did so of that night when he had rubbed the yellow mercury stuff on her hand while she slept.

He did not know whether he had done it from love or hate. But he did know that he did not want to go into the unknown alone.

Poul Anderson

TO PROMOTE THE
GENERAL WELFARE

THE Constitutional Convention had recessed for the mid-winter holidays, and Daniel Coffin returned to his house at Lake Moondance. In this part of the lowlands the season brought roaring, chill rains, winds which streaked along mountains to make forests creak and sough, dazzlements of light and hasty shadow as the cloud deck swirled apart, re-formed, and broke open again upon sun, moons, or stars. To travel by aircar was not predictably safe; thus, custom was for folk to stay home, visit only near neighbors, in revelry draw closer to their kindred.

Last year he had not done do, but had been the guest of Tom and Jane de Smet in Anchor. His place had felt too big and hollow, and at the same time too full of ghosts, Soon afterward, though, his eldest granddaughter Teresa and her husband Leo Svoboda had suggested they move in with him. It was partly kindness to an old man they loved; their dwelling was no mansion like his, but it was comfortable and they were prospering. Yet there were enough mutual practical advantages—such as centralizing control over the vast family holdings, now that improved transportation made it possible—that they were not offending him with charity. He was glad to agree.

Pioneers marry young. However well tamed this region might be, the frontier was far off, that entire planet which

29

beckoned every lowlander on Rustum. Leo and Teresa already had two children, and a third on the way. Again the house resounded to joyous voices, again the lawns knew fleet little bodies of his own blood; and Daniel Coffin regained the happiness which is peace.

Today his household had been trimming the tree. Afterward he felt tired. He wasn't played out, he knew. His hair might be thin and white, the broad face seamed, but his eyes needed no contacts, his stocky frame was erect as ever, and he could walk many a man half his age into the ground. Still, he had overdone it a trifle in romping with the kids. A quiet couple of hours before dinner would let him take full part in its ceremonies and cheer.

He passed slowly through rooms and halls. Much of their serene proportions, blue-gray plastering, gleaming-grained wood floors, furniture and fireplaces, had grown beneath his hands; much of the drapery was Eva's work. Later, when the plantation commanded a large staff and most of their attention, they had hired professionals to enlarge the building. But the heart of it, he thought, would always be the heart that Eva and he had shared.

Upstairs was their suite, bedchamber, bath, and a separate study for each. At first, after she died, he had wanted to close hers off, or make a kind of shrine of it. Later he came to understand how she would have scorned that, she who always looked outward and lived in the overflowingness of tomorrow. He gave it to Teresa for her use and she could make whatever changes she wished.

His private room stayed as it had been, big desk, big leather armchair, walls lined with books as well as microtapes, book publishing having become a flourishing luxury industry well before anyone might have expected it on an isolated colony world. French doors gave on a balcony. The panes were full of rain, wind hooted, lightning flared, thunder made drumfire which shuddered in the walls. He could barely see down a sweep of grass, trees, flowerbed-bordered paths to the great lake. Waves ran furious over its iron hue. Besides the storm, Raksh was at closest approach, raising tides across the tides of the sun.

The apartment was gloomy and a touch cold. He switched on the heater and a single fluoropanel, put Bach's Fifth Brandenburg on the player, poured himself a small whisky and settled down with his pipe and the *Federalist Papers.*

My duty to reread them, if we're trying to work out a government which'll stay libertarian, now that population's reached the point where Rustum needs more than a mayor and council in Anchor, he thought; then, chuckling: *Duty, hell! I enjoy the style. They could write in those days.*

What'd you have said, Washington, Jefferson, Hamilton, Madison, if you'd been told that someday some people would travel twenty light-years, cut themselves off from the planet that begot mankind, just to keep alive the words you lived by?

I suspect you'd say, "Don't copy us. Learn from us—from our mistakes, what we overlooked, as well as what we got right."

We're trying, gentlemen.

"The erection of a new government, whatever care or wisdom may distinguish the work, cannot fail to originate questions of intricacy and nicety—"

Bop, it said on the door. He knew that shy knock. "Come in," he called.

His great-granddaughter entered, "Hi," she said.

"I figured you'd be playing with the other kids, Alice," he answered, referring more to those of the staff than to her younger brother.

"I'm tired, too." The slight form in the crisp white frock snuggled against his trousers. "Story?"

"Calculating minx. Well, c'mon." He helped the girl scramble to his lap. Her eyes were blue and enormous, her curls the color and odor of sunlight—if memory served, exactly like those of Mary Lochaber when she was young. No surprise, considering that Mary was also an ancestor of Alice. . . .

She gave him a happy sigh. "What kind of story do you want?" he asked.

" 'Bout you an' Eva-Granny."

For an instant he *knew* Eva was gone, no more than three years gone, and darkness went through him in a flood. It left;

he could look at her picture on the desk and think how it was good to give this flesh of her flesh what he could of what she had been and done; for then, after he himself, and later the children they had gotten together, were likewise departed, a glow of her would live on.

And it was no longer pain for him, really, it was a special kind of pleasure to hark back.

"Hm-m-m, let me see," he murmured. He blew a series of smoke rings, which made Alice giggle in delight and poke her finger through them as they went by. Images drifted before him, sharper and brighter than anything in this room except the girl and her warmth. Were they truly from so far in the past? That didn't seem believable. Of course, these days time went like the wind. . . .

"Ah, yes," he decided. "You recall I told you how we were explorers before we settled down, Eva-Granny and I."

"Yes. You tol' me 'bout when the t-t-t—TERASAURS," she got out triumphantly, "they went galloop, galloop 'roun' an' 'roun' the big rock till you made'm stop."

"I couldn't have done that without Eva-Granny's help earlier, Alice. Okay, shortly afterward she got the idea of taking a boat out to some islands where nobody had ever landed, only flown over, but that looked wonderful from the air." (The fantastic coraloid formations might give a clue to certain puzzles concerning marine ecology, which in turn were important if fisheries were to develop further. No need to throw these technicalities at the youngster—nor, actually, any truth if he did, as far as her viewpoint went; because Eva and he had really wanted to explore the marvel for its own sake. She was always seeking the new, the untried. When she became a mother and the mistress of a plantation, it had not taken the freshness from her spirit; she originated more ideas, studies, undertakings than he did, and half of his innovations had been sparked by her eagerness.) "In those days there weren't enough motors and things to go around, no, not nearly enough. All the motorboats were being used other places. We kept a sailboat by the sea. It was the same kind, except bigger, as I have on the lake, and, in case you don't know, that's called a sloop."

"Becoss it goes sloop-sloop-sloop inna water?"

Coffin laughed. "Never thought of that! Anyhow—"

The phone bonged: its "urgent" tone. " 'Scuse me, sweetheart," Coffin said, and leaned over to press the accept button.

The screen filled with the features of Dorcas Hirayama, mayor of Anchor and thus president of the Constitutional Convention. Her calm was tightly held. "Why, hello," Coffin greeted. "Happy holidays."

She smiled at the girl on his lap. "Happy holidays, Alice," she said. To Coffin: "I'm afraid you'd better send her out."

He didn't ask the reason, knowing it would prove valid. He simply inquired, "For how long?"

"Shouldn't take more than five minutes to tell. Then I suppose you'll want to spend a while thinking."

"A moment, please." Coffin lowered Alice to the floor, rose, and clasped her hand. "Do you mind, dear?" He didn't see any public question as worth ignoring the dignity of a child. "My Lady Hirayama has a secret. Why don't you take this book—" she crowed in glee as he gave her a photo album from his roving days— "and go look at it in my bedroom? I'll call you as soon as I'm through."

When the door between was shut, he returned to the mayor. "Sorry, Dorcas."

"I'm sorry to interrupt you, Daniel. But this won't wait . . . in spite of going back about thirty-five years."

For several heartbeats he stood moveless. Chills chased along his spine and out to the ends of his nerves. Lightning glared, thunder exploded, rain dashed against the glass.

Thirty-five years. Rustum years. That's about twenty of Earth's. The time it takes light to go between Eridani and Sol.

He sat back down, crossed ankle on knee, tamped the coals in his pipe. "It's happening, then?" he said flatly.

"It has happened. The message was, they planned to launch a colonizing fleet toward us within five years—five of their years. Unless something interfered, and that doesn't seem likely, those ships are, at this moment, a third, maybe almost half of the way here. We may have as much as fifty years before they arrive, but no more and probably less.''

"How many aboard?"

"It's a bigger fleet than carried our founders. The message gave an estimate of five thousand adult passengers."

In the little death of suspended animation, that they entered dreaming of a glorious resurrection on Rustum—

"What do people have to say about this?" Coffin asked.

"The man who read the tape had the sense to come straight to me, thank God. I swore him to silence. You're the first I've talked to."

"Why me?"

Hirayama smiled again, wryly this time. "False modesty never did become you, Daniel. You know how I respect your judgment, and I'm hardly alone in that. Besides, you're the convention delegate from the Moondance region, its leader at home and its spokesman in Anchor, and it's the largest and wealthiest in the lowlands, which makes you the most powerful person off High America and comparable in influence to anybody on it. Furthermore, you know your folk better than a highlander like me, who can't come down among them without a helmet, ever will. Must I continue spelling it out?"

"No need. I'd blush too hard. Okay, Dorcas, what can I do for you?"

"First, give me your opinion. We can't sit on the news more than a few days, but meanwhile we can lay plans and rally our forces. Offhand, what do you suppose the lowland reaction will be?"

Coffin shrugged. "Mildly favorable, because of glamour and excitement and the rest. No more than that. We're so busy overrunning the planet. Nor do five thousand immigrants mean a thing to us, as regards crowding or competition, when we don't yet total a lot more ourselves."

"You confirm my guess, then."

"Besides," Coffin said, not happily, "very few of the newcomers will be able to live down here anyway."

"Doubtless true. The devil's about to break loose on High America, you realize that, don't you?"

"Indeed I do."

"Suggestions?"

34

Coffin pondered before he said: "Let me think at leisure, as you predicted I'd want to. I'll call you back after sleep-time. Agreeable?"

"It's got to be. Well, happy holidays."

"Same to you. Don't let this spoil your fun, Dorcas. You and I won't have to cope with the arrival."

"No. That girl of yours will."

"Right. We'll have to decide on her account. I only hope we're able to. Good-bye."

Coffin switched off, crossed the room, and knocked on the inner door. "All done, Alice," he said. "Shall we continue our story?"

A calm spell, predicted to last a while, enabled Coffin to flit about by aircar, visiting chosen households throughout that huge, loosely defined territory which looked to him for guidance in its common affairs. He could have phoned instead, but the instrument made too many nuances impossible. Nobody objected to his breaking the custom of the season. They were glad to return some of the hospitality he and Eva had shown them.

Thus, he went for a horseback ride with George Stein, who farmed part of the estate whereon he lived but mainly was the owner of the single steel mill in the lowlands, hence a man of weight. Stein knew that Coffin's real desire was to speak privately. Yet the outing was worthwhile in its own right.

The Cyrus Valley was lower and warmer than Lake Moondance. Here many trees and shrubs—goldwood, soar-top, fakepine, gnome—kept their foliage the year around. The blue-green "grasses" of summer had given way to russet muscoid, whose softness muffled hoofbeats. This was open woodland, where groves stood well apart. Between them could be seen an upward leap of mountains, which lost themselves in pearl-gray cloud deck. The air was mild and damp, blowing a little, laden with odors of humus. Afar whistled a syrinx bird.

When Coffin had finished his tale, Stein was quiet for a space. Saddle leather squeaked, muscles moved soothingly between thighs. *A good land*, Coffin thought, not for the first or the hundredth time. *How glad I am that, having conquered it, we made our peace with it. May there always be this kind of restraining wisdom on Rustum.*

"Well, not altogether unexpected, hey?" Stein said at length. "I mean, ever since radio contact was established, it's seemed more and more as if this colony wasn't a dying-gasp attempt after all. Earth's made some resumption of a space effort. And they may have a few expeditions out looking for new habitable planets, as they claim; but they know for certain that ours is."

"On the highlands," Coffin answered redundantly. "I doubt that this lot they're shipping to us, I doubt it contains a bigger percentage than the original settlers had, of persons able to tolerate lowland air pressure. And . . . the highlands are pretty well filled up."

"What? You're not serious, Dan."

"Never more so, my friend. There isn't much real estate that far aloft, and High America contains nearly the whole of what's desirable. Most has been claimed, under the Homestead Rule, and you can bet your nose that the rest soon will be, after this news breaks."

"Why? Who has to worry about getting crowded? The lowlands can feed a hundred High Americas if we expand cultivation. Let them industrialize the whole plateau if need be." Stein lifted a hand. "Oh, yes, I remember past rivalry. But that was before you got some industry started down here. Now we don't have to fear economic domination. Anytime they overcharge us, we can build new facilities and undersell them. Therefore it makes perfectly good sense to specialize along geographical lines."

"The trouble is," Coffin said, "that prospect is exactly what's worrying the more thoughtful High Americans. Has been for quite a while. They've been raised in the same tradition of elbow room and ample unspoiled nature as we have, George. They want to keep it for their descendants; and the area available to those descendants will be limited for a long time, historically speaking, until at last the pressure-tolerant genes have crowded the older kind out of man on Rustum.

36

"For instance, take my sometime partner Tom de Smet. He's spent a fairish part of his life buying out land claims in the wilderness, as he got the money to do it. He's created a really gigantic preserve. He'll deed it to the public, *if* we write into the Constitution an article making its preservation perpetual, and certain other provisions he wants as regards the general environment. Failing that, his family intends to keep it. On a smaller scale, similar things have been happening—similar baronies have been growing—everywhere on High America. People have not forgotten what overpopulation did to Earth, and they don't aim to let their personal descendants get caught in the same bind."

"But—oh, Lord!" Stein exclaimed. "How many immigrants did you say? Five thousand? Well, I grant you even forty years hence, or whenever they arrive, even then they'll be a substantial addition. Nevertheless, a minority group. And no matter how they breed, they won't speed population increase enough to make any important difference."

"They will, though," Coffin replied, "having no land available to them for the reasons I just gave you—they will be a damned significant augmentation of one class of people we're already beginning to get a few of."

"Who?"

"The proletariat."

"What's that?"

"Not everybody on High America succeeded in becoming an independent farmer, a technical expert, or an entrepreneur. There are also those who, however worthy, have no special talents. Laborers, clerks, servants, routine maintenance men, et cetera. Those who have jobs, whatever jobs they happen to get, rather than careers. Those whose jobs get automated out from under them when employers acquire the means to build the machinery—unless they accept low wages and sink to the bottom of the social pyramid."

"What about them?" Stein asked.

"You've not been keeping in touch with developments on High America over the years. I have. Mind you, I'm not scoffing at the people I'm talking about. Mostly they're perfectly decent, conscientious human beings. They were absolutely vital in the early days.

"The point is, the early days are behind us. The frontier on High America is gone. We have a planetful of frontier in the lowlands, but that's no help to men and women who can't breathe here without getting sick.

"Anchor hasn't got a real city proletariat yet, nor has its countryside got a rural one. Nevertheless, the tendency exists. It's becoming noticeable, as increasing numbers of machines and workers end the chronic labor shortage we used to have.

"If something isn't done, Rustum will repeat Earth's miserable history. Poverty-stricken masses. Concentration of wealth and power in the hands of the few. Attempted reforms which amount to the growth of collectivism. Later, demagogues preaching revolution, and many of the well-off applauding, because they no longer have roots either, in a depersonalized society. Upheavals which can only lead to tyranny. Everything which we were supposed to escape by coming to Rustum!"

Stein frowned. "Sounds farfetched."

"Oh, it is farfetched in the lowlands," Coffin admitted. "A territory this big won't stifle in a hurry. But High America is a different case."

"What do they plan to do to head off this, uh, proletariat?"

Coffin smiled, not merrily. "That's a good question. Especially when the whole idea of the Constitutional Convention is to secure individual rights—close the loopholes through which they got shot down in the republics of Earth—limit the government strictly to keeping public order and protecting the general environment—because, thank God, we don't have to worry about foreign enemies." Somberly: "Unless we generate our own. Societies have been known to polarize themselves. Civil wars are common in history."

"On the one hand, then, you don't want a government able to take hold of things; on the other hand, you don't dare let things drift," Stein complained. "What do you propose, then?"

"Nobody has a neat solution," Coffin said. "Besides, we hope to avoid imposing any ideology, unless you count freedom itself. However—official policies could maybe encourage an organic development. For instance, under the 'public order' heading, government might create incentives for employers to treat their employees as human beings, *individual* human beings, not just interchangeable machines or a faceless organized mass. Better conditions could be maintained for the growth of small than big businesses; a strict hard-money rule ought to help there, if it includes some provision for persons down on their luck. On the larger scale, under 'environmental protection,' maybe agreements can be reached which'll distribute economic activity in such ways that everybody will have a chance to get ahead, no matter where he lives. Voluntary agreements, of course, with a profit motive behind them, but entered into under the advice of scholars who see more than just the immediate profit.''

Coffin sighed. ''Those are superficial examples,'' he finished. ''We can't prescribe the behavior of future generations. All we can do is be aware of certain dilemmas, present and future, put forth ideas, and hammer into our successors that they will face the future ones and had better start preparing well in advance.''

Stein rode sunk in thought. Wind lulled, leaves whispered. Two kilometers off, a herd of cerothere left a wood and started across the sward in graceful bounds.

Finally he said: ''I guess I see what you're driving at, Daniel. Forty or fifty years from now, the proletariat problem should still be fairly small. Only a few people, at worst, should be in that uprooted condition. The economy will be expanding, jobs potentially plentiful, lots of surplus wealth which can be used to help the laid-off city worker get on his own feet. Nothing unmanageable, given common sense and good will.

''Except . . . then Earth dumps five thousand newcomers on us.''

Coffin nodded. ''Yes,'' he said.

''Who'll get no chance to become freeholders. Who'll have to adapt to the higher gravity, the longer day and shorter year, a million different matters before they can work. And then they aren't likely to have skills that're in demand, considering how even the simplest things must be done otherwise on Earth. Instead of occasional individuals who need a helping hand once in a while, High America gets an instant proletariat!"

"For which it won't be prepared, George, because it won't have had experience with the type. Shucks, I certainly wouldn't know how best to treat them, and doubt if the most sophisticated Anchor dweller could make a much better guess than mine."

"It'll hardly affect the lowlands."

"Oh, yes, it will, if we want to keep a unified planet." Coffin paused. "Or a free one. Elbow room doesn't guarantee liberty. Some of the harshest empires in Earth history had all kinds of wide-open spaces."

He straightened in the saddle, though he was beginning to feel weariness from a ride that he would once have considered short. "That's why I'm traveling around, talking to influential and respected persons like you," he said. "I've got to have the backing of this community—because I mean to make a damned radical proposal when the convention reopens."

Stein considered his friend for a while before he responded. "I may or may not agree with you, Daniel. Frankly, here is my country, the country I care about, not High America. But I'll hear you out, of course."

And if need be, Coffin thought, *I have reserves of my own to call on.* He began speaking.

The de Smet house, where Coffin stayed when he visited Anchor, lay well out from the center of town, in an area where most homes stood on broad grounds, amidst groves and gardens. Street lamps were infrequent, and trees broke the city's light haze. Thus, there was little to blur the sky when the man from Lake Moondance went for a walk.

Winter on the altiplano had turned silent and cold. The face stung, the body was glad of a thick coverall, breath felt liquid as it entered the nostrils and came back out in stiff white puffs. Where byways were unpaved, the ground rang underfoot. Elsewhere reached snow, frost-glittering until vision faded out in distance and shadowiness. The occasional yellow shining from windows looked infinitely tender but infinitely tiny. Far in the east, the peaks of the Hercules reared glacier-sharp.

Overhead stood heaven. One rarely saw such a wonder in the lowlands, however many other wonders they gave in exchange. Stars crowded the dark, sparks of frozen fire which melted into the Milky Way; tonight that great torrent gleamed like sea-glow. Three sister planets burned in copper, silver, and amber. Among them hastened pygmy Sohrab, while Raksh hung near the half, so low in the west that illusion made it huge, and cast the shadows of trees and drifts long across the land.

Eva had always loved this sight.

The path reached the Emperor River and followed its bank. It sheened hard frozen. On its opposite side, buried fields and pastures rose toward hills and wilderness. Against that remote murk glimmered a few lights, from one of the villages which were springing up across the plateau.

To Coffin, sound seemed muffled in this thin air; and in these his latter years he had grown hard of hearing. He wasn't aware of the skaters until he rounded a bend in the river, screened by a clump of plume oak, and saw them. Here a road was carried by a bridge. Around its piers and across the ice frolicked a score of boys and girls. They whizzed, they swooped, they laid arms about each other's waists and took wing. Their shouting and laughter crackled in the chill.

Coffin went onto the span to watch. Abruptly he noticed another already present. The lad was tall, but not only was he wearing a black outfit, the African share of his ancestry made his face almost invisible at a distance. The skates which he had removed caught the moonlight at his feet.

"Why, . . . hullo," Coffin said, peering.

"Oh." The youth turned. "Mr. Coffin. How do you do, sir?"

The man recognized him, Alex Burns, son of a neighbor of de Smet: a bright, well-mannered chap. "Taking a rest?"

"Not exactly, sir." Alex gripped the railing and stared away. "I got to thinking."

"On a night like this? Seems as if you're missing a lot of fun. Sure wish I could get in on it."

"Really? Sir, you're welcome to borrow my skates."

"Thanks, but at my age, a fall under Rustum gravity can be a serious matter. And I've got business ahead of me."

"Yes, sir. Everybody knows that."

Then Alex swung around again to confront him and said in a desperate voice, "Mr. Coffin, could I talk with you?"

"Certainly. Though I don't know what a rusticating gaffer like me has to say that'd be of use." *Yet I remember my sons at your age—how short a while ago!*

"This news . . . about the fleet coming from Sol—it's true?" Somehow the adolescent squeak in midquestion was not ridiculous.

"As far as we can tell. Twenty light-years between makes for slow communications. The Earth government may have changed its mind meanwhile. They were phasing out space travel when your ancestors left. Too costly, given a bloated population pressing on resources worn thin. Not quite in their world view, either: The culture was turning more and more from science and technology to mysticism and ceremony."

"Th-that's what my teachers say. Which is how come I'm scared this is a, a false alarm."

"Well, I don't think it'll turn out to be. Giving the Constitutionalists passage to Rustum was a gimmick to get rid of them. But those who elected to go weren't all the Constitutionalists by any means, nor was that the only kind of dissenter. Once we started sending messages back, our example seems to've had considerable psychological effect, roused a widespread desire to emulate. My suspicion is, the government has no choice except to resume a space effort—for several decades, at least, till the social climate changes again. They claim they're searching for other habitable planets. . . . No, I think this emigrant fleet is indeed under weigh."

"Why don't our people want it?"

The anguish startled Coffin. "Well, uh, well, some folks worry about the effects on society. That's not unanimous,

42

Alex. I assure you, the average lowlander has nothing against receiving a few thousand newcomers."

"But the, the average High American—"

"Nobody's taken a poll. I'm not sure, myself, how a vote on the question would go."

Alex flung an arm skyward, pointing. The constellations of Rustum were scarcely different from those of Earth; in this universe, twenty light-years are the single stumbling step of an infant. But just above Boötes flickered a wanness which was Sol.

"Th-they can come to us," the boy stammered. "Why can't we go to them?"

"We haven't the industry to build spacecraft. Won't for generations, maybe centuries."

"And meanwhile we have to stay here! Our whole lives!" Did tears catch the level moonbeams?

Now Coffin understood. "How does your pressure tolerance test out?" he asked softly.

"I can live . . . down to about . . . t-t-two kilometers below."

"That's not bad. Plenty of territory in that range. You can have an adventurous life if you want."

"Oh, yes, sir. I s'pose."

"As I recall, you aim to become a scientist. Well, there's no lack of field research left to do. And if you want to go further down, clear to sea level, why, the new-model air helmets are excellent."

"It's not the same." Alex gulped, knotted fists at sides, and after a while said rapidly: "Please don't think I'm whining, sir. Nor am I, uh, uh, looking down on anybody. But most lowlanders I've met—you're different, of course—most of them, I don't . . . well, we don't fight or anything, but we don't seem to have a lot to talk about."

Coffin nodded. "The frontier doesn't exactly breed intellectuals, does it? Do bear in mind, though, son: those scouts, lumberjacks, farmers, fishermen—they aren't stupid. They simply have different concerns from this tamed High America. In fact, the well-established lowland communities, like my Lake Moondance, they no longer maintain the frontier personality either.''

No, instead it's a wealth-conscious squirearchy, a yeomanry settling down into folkways—not effete, not ossified . . . still, we've become rather ingrown and self-satisfied, haven't we? It hasn't been so on my plantation; Eva never allowed it to become so. She got the kids, and me, to lift our eyes from our daily concerns. Elsewhere, however—No, I hardly think Alex would find many of his own sort around Lake Moondance.

''The compromise for you,'' he suggested, ''might be to do your field work in company with roughneck local guides —who can be top-notch company, remember; who *are* if you take them on the proper terms—and afterward you come back here and write up your findings, where people are cultured.''

''Culture!'' Alex fleered. ''They think 'culture' means playing the same symphonies and reading the same books their grandfathers did!''

''That's not entirely fair. We have artists, authors, composers, not to mention scientists, doing original work.''

''How original? The science is . . . using tried and true methods, never basic research . . . and the arts copy the old models, over and over—''

He speaks considerable truth, Coffin thought.

Alex's finger stabbed back at the stars. ''If they really were original, sir,'' he cried, ''they wouldn't want to wall us off from those. Would they?''

Coffin consoled him as well as might be.

It was doubtful if man would ever altogether outlive the heritage of the planet which bore him. He could train himself to some degree of change from the ancient rhythm of her turning, but not enough to become a fully diurnal creature on Rustum. In the middle latitude at which Anchor lay, a midwinter night lasted for forty-two hours. Of necessity, during two fourteen-hour segments of that darkness, indoor and outdoor illumination made the town a cluster of small suns.

Beneath this sky-hiding roof of light, delegates to the second session of the Constitutional Convention mounted the staircase into Wolfe Hall. They numbered about fifty men and women. Though all were dressed to show due respect for the occasion, the costumes were nearly as varied as the ages. (Daniel Coffin was the oldest, the youngest a male who probably didn't shave oftener than once a day.) Here a professor walked lean and dignified, in tunic and trousers as gray as his head but the academic cloak gorgeous on his shoulders. There an engineer had reverted to archaic styles and put upon herself a long skirt of formality. Yonder a sea captain, weathered and squint-eyed, rolled forward in billed cap and brass buttons, next to the blue uniform of an air pilot. A rancher from lowland North Persis, otherwise a sensible man, flaunted leather garments and a necklace of catling teeth. The physician with whom he talked had underlined her standing in the cut of her jacket. . . . Coffin felt drab among them. And yet, he thought, weren't they reaching a bit, weren't they being just a touch too studiedly picturesque?

Citizens crowded the pavement, watching, in an eerie hush. Anchor had grown used to seeing the congress assemble. But this time was different. This time its first order of business was light-years remote and terrifyingly immediate. Soon they would hasten home, to follow the proceedings on television. Afterward they would argue in their houses, fields, shops, laboratories, camps, schools, taverns, and who knew what passions might flare?

Coffin paused in the lobby to leave his coverall. Most others had omitted that garment, as being too unsolemn when they scrambled in or out of it, and walked in frozen dignity from their lodgings. Low-voiced talk buzzed around him. An ache throbbed in his left wrist; probably he needed an arthritis booster. He shoved the awareness aside and concentrated on his plan of action. He must get his licks in early, because he hadn't the stamina any longer for ten or twelve unbroken hours of debate. Well, he and Dorcas Hirayama had discussed this privately beforehand.

The building had been enlarged over the years, but the meeting place was the original whole of it, piously preserved birch wainscoting and rough rafters. Echoes boomed. Fold-ing chairs spread across the floor. At the far end rose the platform, decorated in red-white-and-blue bunting, Freedom Flag on the wall behind—the platform where for three generations, speakers had spoken, actors performed, orchestras played, callers sounded the measures of square dances.

For an instant the assembly was gone from around Daniel Coffin. They were calling a new one, and he and Mary Lochaber ran hand in hand, laughterful like skaters, to join in, and afterward he would walk her home under stars and moons.

No. That was then. Mary married Bill Sandberg, and I married Eva Spain, and this was best for us both, and at last we were united in Alice and David. I'm sorry, Eva.

It was as if he heard her chuckle and felt her rumple his hair.

Well—The delegates were taking their seats, much scraping and muttering back and forth. Hirayama was mounting the podium. The cameramen were making final adjustments. Coffin shivered. *Poor heating in here. Or else simply that old blood runs cold.* His head lifted. *They may find it can still run pretty hot when it wants to.*

The gavel slammed. How far back did that signal go, anyway? To the first cave patriarch whose stone hammer smote a log? There was strength in the thought, a sense of not being utterly adrift and alone in time. No wonder the colonists tried so hard to keep Earth ways alive, or actually to revive some which had been as obsolete on Earth as the liberty their ancestors came here to save. And when this failed on a world that was not Earth, no wonder they were so quick to develop rituals and taboos of their own.

"In the name of the people of Rustum, for whom we are gathered, I call this meeting to order," said the clear female voice. It continued through parliamentary formalities to which nobody really listened, not even those who took part.

Until:

"As you doubtless know, we've had a surprise dropped in our laps." Coffin felt his mouth twitch upward. Now Dorcas could start behaving like herself! She leaned forward, hands on the lectern, small in her gown but large in her presence.

46

"Maybe it's best that it did occur at this precise time. In writing the basic law of our planet, we'll remember that a universe encloses it.

"At any rate, many persons, including many members of this assembly, feel we should take the matter up before going on to our regular agenda. I agree. By virtue of the powers vested in me, et cetera, I've appointed a couple of committees to study the implications of the immigrant fleet and make recommendations. This will be kept brief, ladies and gentlemen. No general discussion. The idea is to set forth different views as clearly as possible, then adjourn to consider them, then reconvene to exchange thoughts in detail.

"Will Dr. O'Malley's committee please report first?"

Only their chairman joined her. He'd probably domineered over everyone else, for the stiff, plainly clad, middle-aged man had to that extent inherited the personality of his grandfather. *However, Jack O'Malley made his domineering fun*, Coffin remembered from boyhood. *Also, . . . well, I'm not saying Morris O'Malley is inferior; but a lab administrator is not the same as an explorer who could drink his whole band under the table and wake in six hours, hound-dog eager to go discover some new miracle.*

The speaker rustled papers. "My lady and colleagues, perhaps it would be best if I commence by summarizing the situation as my group understands it," he said, and did at a length which caused Hirayama to drum nails on the arm of her chair.

"Well." Finally O'Malley's tone grew vigorous. "The question before us is twofold. Should we allow the travelers to join us? If not, can we prevent it?

"The second part is simple. We can. Presumably the fleet is already en route. Theron Svoboda, chief of interstellar communications, thinks we have a fair chance of intercepting it with a maser beam, getting a message through to the officers on watch. These can change course for a different star or, more likely, return to the Solar System.

"If this fails and the ships arrive, we—rather, the next generation of us—will nevertheless be in full control. A minority of your committee advocates constructing nuclear missiles to ensure it. The majority considers that would be a waste of effort. Fuel requirements being what they are, those are surely unarmed vessels. They will depend on us to help them refine reaction mass for the trip home. In no case can a few bewildered newcomers impose their will on a planet.''

He paused for a sip of water. "Very well. The issue is, therefore, *should* we give entry to these self-invited strangers?

"They bring us no benefit. We'd have to nurse them through adjustment to Rustum; for certainly we could never let them suffer and die as horribly as did many among our forefathers, whom nobody helped. Later we'd have to take time we can ill afford to teach them the habits, technicalities, and tricks which generations on Rustum have painfully learned for themselves. And at the end, in reward, what would we get? Workers not especially desirable, being grossly limited in what they can do. Perhaps not workers at all, but mere parasites. I shall return to this point shortly.

"We are under no moral obligation to admit them. Your committee has reviewed every tape of every communication between Earth and Rustum A few from our side may have waxed overenthusiastic. But no government of ours has ever issued any invitation or given any promises—if only because hitherto we have never possessed a very formally organized government.

"If they are turned back, none but their officers on watch will even have looked upon the Promised Land. The human cargo would remain in suspended animation until reawakened in Earth orbit or, conceivably, in orbit around some wholly new planet. If they feel disappointment, why, so must every human being, often in this life.

"We have the power to exclude them, and we have the right. Your committee finds that we have, in addition and ultimately, the duty to exclude them.''

Coffin heard out the argument against allowing a proletariat to appear overnight. He wasn't surprised to find it almost identical with the position he'd outlined to George Stein and others. O'Malley was an intelligent man in his way, and knew history. . . . Coffin felt his lips quirk afresh.

You've got a moderately good opinion of yourself, don't you, Daniel, my boy?

He tensed when O'Malley went on, because here he recognized, not an abstract sociological argument, but that which reached into the guts and grabbed.

"More vital, ladies and gentlemen, people of Rustum, far more vital is what I next have to say. Dare we open our gates to a gang of aliens?"

O'Malley let silence underline that before he continued. "Your committee does not necessarily denigrate anyone's human worth," he said; and Coffin thought that the measured syllables, the overtone of regret, were the best oratory he'd heard in years. "Assuredly we do not subscribe to any cruel and absurd doctrine of racial hierarchies." He bowed a little toward Hirayama, toward Gabriel Burns, toward the entire room and planet. "If we are of predominantly Caucasoid North American stock, we are not exclusively that, and we are proud that in us lives the entire human species.

"But"—he lifted a finger—"it would be equally absurd and, in the long run, equally cruel, to pretend that *cultures* do not differ in basic ways. And let us hear no bleat that there can be no value judgments between them. The freedom we enjoy is superior to the despotism on Earth; the rational judgment we cultivate is superior to, yes, more truly human than the blind obedience and blinder faith which have overwhelmed Earth.

"People of Rustum, it is all too easy for us to imagine that the thousands on their way here are just like our forebears—perhaps not the same in color of skin or shape of eyelids, but the same inside, where it counts. Were this true, we might hope to prevent them from becoming proles, difficult though that would be.

"But consider. Earth has not been static since our founding fathers made their weary pilgrimage hither. Study the transcribed communication tapes for yourselves, people of Rustum. Judge for yourselves how social evolution back there seems to have nearly obliterated the last shards of American—no, Western civilization—those shards which

49

we mean to preserve and to make the foundation of a new and more enduring house of liberty.

"Today's emigrants are not in search of freedom. That notion is extinct on Earth. They are apparently dissenters, but their dissent is not that of the individual demanding a steel-clad bill of rights. What they seek, that puts them in conflict with their authorities, is not certain. It appears to be a kind of neo-Confucianism, though with paradoxical ecstatic elements. Who can tell? When seventy years must pass between question asked and reply received, there can be no real understanding.

"The point is, they are alien.

"Shall we, who still dwell precariously on a world that is still full of deadly surprises, shall we take upon ourselves such a burden of unassimilable outsiders?"

O'Malley lowered his voice. Almost, it tolled into the hush: "Would that actually be a kindness to the outsiders themselves? I have pointed out that they are a potential poverty class. I will now point out that since they are alien, since there are bound to be offenses and clashes, they could become the victims of hatred, even outright persecution. We are not saints on Rustum. We are not immune to the ancient diseases of xenophobia, callousness, legalized robbery, and mob violence. Let us not inflict upon our home the same unhealable wound which was inflicted on Mother America.

"Lead us not into temptation."

He stepped down to such applause, from the mostly high-lander congress, that Hirayama could barely be heard: "We will take a half hour's recess."

Coffin stood with his pipe, though smoke had scant taste in air this keen, on an upstairs balcony. Anchor gleamed and murmured beneath, busy at its work, its hopes. Its radiance dimmed, in his vision, the ice on the river, the reaching snowlands, the peaks and the stars above them. *But I only have to walk a few kilometers out*, he thought, *and I'll be alone with the inhuman and its eternity.*

I'm also close to them in time, of course, his mind added. *Soon I'll be among them.* It was a strange feeling.

A voice brought him around. "Ah, greetings, Daniel. Did you too want to escape the crowd?"

He saw Morris O'Malley's ascetic visage between the street lamps and the moons. "Yes," he replied; the mist of his words fled away into night. "Say, that was a fine speech you made. To be quite frank, better than I expected."

The other man smiled. "Thanks. I'm no Demosthenes. But when you speak from conviction, it gets easier."

"Those are your beliefs?"

"Of course. I have no personal ax to grind. I may live to see that fleet arrive, but before the trouble becomes acute, I'll be safe in my grave. It's my grandchildren I'm worried about."

"Do you really think they'll have that much grief from a bunch of well-meaning Asians or Africans or whatever those are? This is a whole planet, Morris."

O'Malley's voice turned bleak. "For your kind it is."

"It was for your granddad too, in spite of his having to wear a reduction helmet—one of those primitive muscle-powered jobs—every time he ventured below three kilometers."

"He helped map the lowlands. He didn't live in them. We, confined to High America—" The talk he had given made it less astonishing than it would formerly have been, that dry Dr. O'Malley laid a hand on Coffin's shoulder. "Daniel, I know I was oversimplifying. I know the issues are much more subtle and complicated, with far more ifs and maybes. That's precisely what scares me."

Coffin drank smoke and looked across rooftops. "Your granddad never let anything scare him, permanently anyway, that I know of."

"Things were different then. Simple issues of survival."

"I have a notion that, at bottom, all issues are alike. They turn on the same principles. And, for your information, survival wasn't always a simple either-or question."

O'Malley was mute for a while before he said low: "I'm told you're to speak immediately after recess."

Coffin dipped his head. "It won't take as long or be near as eloquent as yours, Morris."

How many of their faces he knew! There was the mother of Leo Svoboda, there the son of Mary Sandberg, there his old poker opponent Ray Gonzales, there young Tregennis who'd worked for him before seeking a fortune in the western islands, there his and Eva's son Charlie whom Tom and Jane de Smet had raised because he couldn't live in the lowlands, his own hair grizzled. . . . Rustum was mystery and immensity, to this day; but man on Rustum remained a world very small and close and dear to itself.

"This is not exactly a committee report," Coffin said. "I represent the Moondance area, and because we thereabouts have reached a sort of consensus, I asked leave of the president to set our views before you."

His throat felt rough. Like his predecessor, he took a drink. He recognized the water; its faint iron tang brought him back to springs near the farm on the Cleft edge when he was a child. How much of everything he had known could he hope to pass on?

"I'll try to be brief," he said, "because my esteemed colleague Dr. O'Malley has covered the generalities, leaving the practicalities to me. Mind you, philosophy and theory are essential. Without them, we blunder blind at best, we're brutes at worst. But they are not ends in themselves; that'd make them mere parlor games. They are guides to action. Life depends on what we *do*—or don't do.

"Shall we or shall we not receive strangers into our midst? I propose we answer the question fast, in practical terms, and get on with our proper business."

He had them, he saw. He was no longer an old man allowed to drone on a while out of respect for what he had been; suddenly he gripped reality in the sight of them all.

"As for the problem that'd be created for High America if we admit outsiders," he said, taking advantage of his lack of oratorical ability to convey a sense of unemotional confidence: "Many of you have been assuming that the highlanders would have to cope with it alone. Why should we lowlanders care? If so, I can sympathize with highlanders who want to use the majority they still will have when the ships come, to forbid them to land any passengers.

"Well, I am here to tell you that Lake Moondance and environs, clear through the Cyrus Valley, does care and wants to help." He heard the breath sigh into fifty pairs of lungs. No doubt it was doing so around the planet. Inwardly, he grinned. Half his effort had gone toward keeping this revelation secret, that he might spring it tonight for top effect.

The other half had gone into argument, cajolery, chicanery, and genteel bribery, to get the support that he must have.

"I expect our sister lowland communities will follow suit," he continued, thereby going a ways toward committing them. "Frontiersmen are generally pragmatists. They have ideals, but their first thought is what material measures will put those ideals to work.

"In this case, the practical problem is that High America would find it difficult, maybe impossible, from both an economic and a social viewpoint, to take in five thousand persons of exotic background, who can't scatter across the globe and get absorbed, but must stay here where they can breathe."

Coffin reached for pipe and tobacco pouch. He didn't really want a smoke this soon after the last; but the homely action of filling the bowl should help bring everything down to a less giddily exalted plane.

"Now that ought to be solvable," he drawled. "As for the cost, why, Moondance is ready to pay a fair share in money, materials, labor, whatever is needed that we can supply. I repeat, I'm sure the other lowland communities will join us in that. Shared, the expense won't fall hard on anybody.

"And you know, that'll be an important precedent, a symbol and function of our unity. I hate to contradict Dr. O'Malley's noble disclaimer, but the fact is, we do have basic differences among us, not only social but actually genetic, racial. Some of us can live down there, some cannot. We must find as much common human ground as we can, to transcend that. Don't you agree?"

After a wait: " 'Common human ground' includes the good old Homo sapiens' habit of not meekly adapting to circumstances, but grabbing them by the ears and adapting them to us.

"Look, air helmets have improved beyond belief since I was young. Why, when I was a baby they didn't exist! Who says we must stop here? Who says we can't work out some-thing better, a biochemical treatment maybe, which'll let every man, woman, and child on Rustum live anywhere that he or she likes?"

The assembly stirred and exclaimed. He cut through the noise:

"Moondance proposes a joint research effort, which will itself be another unifying element, an effort to discover means of overcoming the handicap that most of our children are born with. I know that's been daydreamed about for a long time. Part of the reason nothing's happened has been that close cooperation of both human breeds is obviously essential, and we lowlanders, at least, have had no motiva-tion toward it, especially with so much else to keep us busy. Tonight we do urge moving from daydream to reality.

"If we succeed in that, the problems associated with admitting immigrants will become trivial. Furthermore, if we commit ourselves to an open-door policy, then the know-ledge that yonder fleet is aimed at us will be one hell of a stimulus to solving this merely scientific problem!"

Again he drank, before he added mildly, "Of course, without that open-door policy, the lowlanders will have no reason to help in such a project, or to promise to help bear the burden if the project fails. If you vote to close the gates, then to hell with you. Stay up here in the isolation you like so much."

Uproar. Dorcas Hirayama hammered for order. As the racket died, a voice from the middle of the room shouted, "Why do you want a lot of damn foreigners?"

Coffin lit his pipe. "I was coming to that," he said, "impolitely though the question may have been put.

"Whether or not we can crack the air-pressure barrier, we can't expect to assimilate the immigrants quickly or easily. To some extent, probably we can never assimilate them at all, in the sense of making them or their descendants identical with us. Besides the obstacles raised by their unfamiliarity with Rustum, why, they're coming here to preserve a way of life, not lose it in a melting pot.

"As said, I think with some sacrifice by both highlands and lowlands, whatever happens otherwise, we can avoid creating a proletariat. At worst, we'll have to tide over the older generation, and make some economic-industrial changes to accommodate the younger one.

"But as for that second aspect Dr. O'Malley discussed— the introduction of foreign philosophies, minds strange to our own—"

He laid down his pipe. He filled his lungs and roared across the hall, echoes thunderous even in his deaf ears:

"God damn it, that's exactly what we need!"

And afterward, into their shock, himself most gently:

"Not many hours ago, I stood on North Bridge and talked to a very puzzled and embittered young man. He couldn't comprehend why his elders wanted to cut us off from the stars. We ended by considering ways and means whereby Rustum might acquire those spaceships when they arrive.

"Unlikely, of course. The point is, the news had made him realize how suffocated he is in this smug backwater we've become. Oh, yes, we have big jobs ahead of us. But who will do them? People exactly like us? If so, what'll there be afterward, except sitting back and admiring the achievements of the ancestors?

"I'll tell you what there'll be. Hell to pay!

"I've heard a great deal of worry expressed about creating a rootless, impoverished proletariat, with no stake or interest in continuing the society that bred it. Ladies and gentlemen, have you considered the danger in creating a proletariat of the soul?

"*Let* foreigners in. Welcome unexpected insights, weird ways, astonishing thoughts and feelings. We may not always like them—probably we often won't—but we'll experience them and they'll make us look to the foundations of our own beliefs. If there's anything at all to the idea of liberty and individual worth, which we're supposed to be keeping alive, then on the whole, we'll be the better for being challenged.

55

And it works two ways, you know. They'll learn from us. Together, the old and the new dweller on Rustum will do and think what neither alone could dream."

Coffin drew breath. He had gotten a little dizzy from so much talking. Sweat was on his skin and his knees shook.

He finished hoarse-voiced: "As most of you know, seeing how I brag about them, I have a couple of great-grandchildren. I don't want to protect them from the cosmos, any more than that boy I met wants to be protected.

"No, they deserve better."

When, after lunations, the debates were ended, the hard bargains driven, the resolution drawn and passed, the law established that Rustum would greet and help the offspring of Earth—

Daniel Coffin sat alone in his room in the de Smet house. He had turned off the fluoros. Moonlight streamed through an open window, icy as the air. Afar reached the taut silence of winter night, barely disturbed by a rumble from the river, whose hardness had begun to break into floes under a first faint flowing of spring.

The coldness touched Eva's portrait on a table. He picked it up. His hand trembled. He was very tired; it would be good to lie down and rest.

"Sweetheart," he whispered. "I wish you could have seen." He shook his head, ran fingers through his hair. *Maybe you did? I don't know.*

"You see," he told his memory of her, "I did what I did because that was what you'd have wanted. Only because of you."

Chad Oliver

CARAVANS UNLIMITED:
MONITOR

THE young warrior was stretched out on the hard, unyielding ground. There was no shade. The burning sun scorched the arid land. The cattlelike hondari shuffled around slowly, without energy, searching out the sparse clumps of brown grass. Yellow dust hung in the still air like an unmoving grainy cloud.

The warrior was on his back, just resting. His head was supported by a special wooden stool under his neck. The purpose of this was to avoid disturbing his elaborate hairdo. The hair was long, coiled into ringlets, and greased with a dull red dressing.

The warrior did not move. Every fold of his dusty loose-fitting cloak was artfully arranged. The garment was the same color as his hair.

His spear was on the ground beside him. It had an iron point and a wooden shaft. It was as long as he was.

The dry air buzzed with flies. They were big ones, drawn by the hondari herds. They were also attracted by the grease in the warrior's hair.

A fly landed on the warrior's forehead. It poked around for a moment and then walked down across his open eyeball.

The warrior blinked his eye, once. Otherwise, he did not move. It was beneath his dignity to notice a fly. Besides, a rapid movement would have disturbed the symmetry of his cloak.

"How *about* that," Alex Porvenir said with admiration.

Martin Ashtola wiped the sweat from his forehead. He was not much impressed. "I'm sure there is considerable potential in these people," he said. "But these men seem so—what is the word? Foppish?"

Alex Porvenir tugged at the brim of his hat to shield his face from the glare of the reddish sun. He fished out his pipe, filled it with hopefully moist tobacco, and took a long time lighting it. He resisted the impulse to lecture the younger man. "The Kwosa *are* vain. Also arrogant, proud, and stubborn—among other things. But don't sell them short until you know them."

Martin Ashtola shrugged. "You're the expert." His tone was faintly insulting. He resented his own lack of authority and his irritation showed. "I hope your plan is a good one. These people aren't much use to us the way they are. All they're interested in is cows—cows and their own beautiful bodies."

Alex wasn't certain whether or not he was glad that Martin was speaking English. He occasionally had euphoric visions of Martin with a spear sticking in him. "As a matter of fact," he said gently, "Caravans was at one time at a loss as to what to offer the Kwosa in trade. They are very self-sufficient; it's one thing that makes them independent. They have to move with their herds of hondari, so they don't go in much for bulky possessions. It was hand mirrors that turned the trick. They like to admire themselves."

The younger man did not respond. He wasn't interested in the business problems of Caravans and he didn't give much of a damn about the psychology of the Kwosa. His blue UN Observer's uniform was getting stained with sweat. He wanted to get back to the ship and talk about Plans. He was very big on Plans. "What do we do now?"

Alex puffed on his pipe. "Wait."

"Wait for what?"

"Wait until our friend finishes his siesta."

"And then?"

"Then we tag along with him as long as he doesn't object. He knows that the sky traders are peculiar people; he'll make allowances."

"What will he *do?*"

"Take the herd to water. Then graze them back to camp where they can be guarded at night. If there's a raid, it will likely come after dark. Besides, camp is where the girls are. He's not all duded up for nothing, you know."

"Why go through all that? You've seen it a hundred times."

Alex smiled. "Yes, but *you* haven't."

"I didn't come here to study these people."

"Why *did* you come? It certainly wasn't at my invitation," Alex wanted to say. He said: "You can't report on my plan unless you know what it is. I can't tell you my plan until you understand the Kwosa."

Martin Ashtola sighed. This wasn't going the way he had figured at all. "Can't we stir Sleeping Beauty into a little action?"

"I wouldn't advise it. He'll get up in his own good time. Surely I don't have to remind *you* about the law. We can't interfere with these people against their will and contrary to their own best interests. He's perfectly happy and doing his job. Let him alone."

The two men waited. Alex Porvenir was patient; he was used to this. He enjoyed being out in the open, hot as it was. It restored him. Martin Ashtola was fretful and decidedly uncomfortable. He was accustomed to the comforts of Earth.

The red sun of Lalande, more than eight light-years from the sun Earth knew, dipped slowly toward the flat horizon. Short shadows striped the grassy plain.

Quite suddenly, the warrior stood up. He did it in one fluid motion. He patted his cloak into place and picked up his spear.

He whistled, sharply. The whistle was shrill between his carefully filed teeth.

The hondari herd strung out and began to move. Horns tossed in the sunlight. The dust grew thicker.

The warrior smiled proudly. "Are they not beautiful?" he

asked in the liquid language of the Kwosa.

"They are hondari," Alex said in the ritual response. "They are beyond beauty."

Martin Ashtola, of course, did not understand what the man had said. He did not, in fact, share in the mystique of the cows. Although livestock were extinct on Earth, except in the zoos he had never bothered to visit, he had no romantic notions about animals. He was a very civilized man.

Alex himself was not unduly thrilled by the hondari herds. They were skinny beasts, all bones and leather. But he understood the feeling that the Kwosa had for the hondari. If he could not share it, he could nevertheless appreciate it.

To the Kwosa, the hondari *were* beautiful.

That was enough.

The two men paced along in the choking yellow dust, following the warrior who followed his herd. Alex could almost smell the water that waited for them.

It was old, he thought. Old for Lalande II, older still for Earth. A man and his herd. Heat, dust, the promise of water. A camp waiting, and food, and women. A spear in your hand, confidence in your heart. Sometimes, the old ways had value. He could have been a Kwosa, rather than what he was. . . .

He shook his head. There was no way to erase his own heritage even had he really wanted to do so. He was an outsider here, as always—

He concentrated on just keeping up with the herd.

The animals were lowing now. They knew the trail. They knew where the water was.

When they reached the shallow stream, the hondari were positively well-mannered. Alex was always surprised by their orderly behavior. There was no stampede, no crowding. According to some invisible status heirarchy, the animals fanned out along the bank and waded in to drink. When the first ones had finished, the second line went in.

After all the hondari had swallowed their fill, the men could drink. They got as far upstream as possible, waded in, and submerged their heads in the water. That is, that was the procedure for Alex and Martin Ashtola. The warrior was far more dainty, not wishing to disturb his hairdo. He simply scooped up water in his hands and sipped. He didn't need much.

The water was not cold but it was cool. It even seemed reasonably clean, but Alex took a pill to be on the safe side. The wetness from his dripping hair felt great against his sunburned neck.

The warrior whistled. The herd moved out, headed back for camp. It was a long way, but the animals were livelier now.

The warrior walked proudly, admiring his own shadow on the land. He carried his spear as though it were a feather. His eyes were alert and watchful. His attitude said plainly that he could handle anything, and would welcome the opportunity.

Alex was not quite so filled with energy, but he felt pretty good. The water had helped, and the sun was losing some of its impact now.

He watched Martin Ashtola out of the corner of his eye.

The younger man was bushed, but he was through complaining. That was a healthy sign.

Alex let it all sink in, savoring it. The patient herd, the warrior, the fading sun, the tough grass. There was a small breeze now and the dust was not so bad.

Alex knew a kind of peace. He was attracted by this life. It was hard, direct, simple, and rewarding. It was free of doubts.

Or perhaps it was only free. . . .

He studied his companion and he willed his silent thoughts.

Watch. See. Feel. Understand.

The great lightship hung in orbit, suspended in the blackness that surrounded Lalande II. The symbol of the laden camel on its bow marked the ship as belonging to Caravans, Unlimited. The camel seemed to be looking down, down into the night, down to where the dusty trails wound across the arid plains. . . .

Alex Porvenir poured himself a libation of Scotch, sat back in his comfortable chair, and thought about Martin Ashtola.

He could thank the Others for Martin Ashtola.

When he and Tucker Olton had discovered the tracks of an alien civilization fooling around with the Lupani on Sirius XI, they had opened a real can of worms. Alex had known that things would never be the same again, but he hadn't expected Martin Ashtola.

It was all perfectly logical, though.

Earth was a strange world, a planet of vast technological expertise that had somehow lost its heart and its vision. With a universe before it, it had elected to contemplate its own rather humdrum navel. There were reasons, of course, but then there are always reasons.

The exploration of the universe had been left in the hands of private trading companies. The UN set up an ET Council that hemmed them in with rules and regulations; the UN was determined that there would be no exploitation of native peoples on other worlds. There was one rule that was never broken: No tax revenues were "squandered" in space.

So far, so good.

The trading companies like Caravans managed to make enough of a profit to keep them going, working the interstellar trade routes through the gray wastes of not-space. They did it by searching out products that were unavailable on Earth and setting up an elaborate marketing and advertising network. It wasn't easy. You had to find the product first. You had to ensure a stable supply. You had to transport it. And you had to make the consumers *want* it; the costs were literally astronomical, and a few mistakes could put you out of business.

It worked. The integrity of the lifeways of other peoples was respected, and if the regulations were sometimes bent a little it was never to the detriment of native cultures.

And Earth had a toehold in space. . . .

But then it happened, the thing that Alex had always both anticipated and feared.

On the world of Arctica, among a people called the Lupani, the traders met the Others. Not exactly *met* them, perhaps, but received their calling card. Another civilization, an alien civilization, operating in space. The Others—

whoever or whatever they might be. Manipulating cultures ruthlessly, changing them, moving them like pawns in some mysterious galactic game of chess.

They had a plan, a design of some sort.

And it could only be aimed, ultimately, at Earth. There was no other civilization that had ventured outward to the stars.

That altered the situation. When the report reached Earth, there was a kind of hysteria for a few weeks. It was not comfortable to be a target of unknown forces.

But there was no *immediate* danger.

There had been no *overt* threat.

And whatever might happen was far in the future—

And the tax money was needed at home—

And so the response Earth made was Martin Ashtola and his counterparts on other ships.

It was not a very heroic or imaginative response. But it was *so* inexpensive.

Just send an Observer out on each trading ship. Give him a title and a nice uniform. It created a kind of instant space navy, and it cost almost nothing.

There was only one small problem.

What did the Observer *do?*

Well, he would observe, obviously. He would report back. He would Keep In Touch, within the dubious limits of interstellar communications.

But beyond that?

Earth had no plan of action, really. It did not even have the data upon which a realistic plan might be based. Instead, the UN ET Council had what amounted to a gut reaction, a vague conviction. It was never stated in so many words. It consisted of a feeling. Its essence was the notion that Earth needed allies, and the stronger the allies were the better.

It was absolute nonsense, of course.

But the human animal was only sporadically rational, to say nothing of wise. He had a tendency to flounder around a bit.

And there was the awkward fact that the basic law under which the trading companies operated prohibited overt cultural manipulation without the consent of the peoples involved.

Martin Ashtola was not frustrated without cause.

Neither was Alex Porvenir.

But Alex had been at this game for a long time. He had seen what there was to see. He knew what he was doing. And he had a few ideas of his own.

That gave him a certain advantage.

He stood up and lit his pipe.

A tall man, Alex. Tall and lean and hard. He was pushing fifty now, but he had taken care of himself. There was some gray in his hair—Helen said that he looked distinguished when she wanted to needle him a little—but his sharp brown eyes were not the eyes of an old man. He still had a stubborn jaw and there was nothing wrong with his reflexes.

His brain still worked, too.

He hoped that he had enough left in the tank for the job ahead.

If not—

The lightships of Caravans did not operate according to some grand design. Martin Ashtola was a complicating factor, a nuisance, but he was not responsible for the visit to Lalande II.

The problem was a simple one. Alex Porvenir had spent a lifetime untangling similar snarls.

The Kwosa were a seminomadic people, shifting about within their territory according to the requirements of the hondari herds. Herders of large stock animals tended to be much alike wherever they were found. Herds were always tempting targets; they were relatively easy to rustle and a man could become wealthy or a pauper overnight. The hondari had to be herded by warriors for protection; there was an endless cycle of raid and counterraid between neighboring tribes. The men were proud, tough, and vain. They had to be. It was a strongly male-oriented society. The women had little to do; they did not need to labor perpetually as they did among farming tribes. They had a notable lack of economic power, since the hondari herds were owned and controlled by the men.

Sex was the great pastime of the Kwosa. It was almost as important as raiding or admiring the hondari. The young men strutted and made themselves beautiful. The girls gasped at the bravery of the warriors and made themselves readily available.

The elders took care of the government when they were old enough to want to slow down a trifle. There came a time, even for a Kwosa, when a nice bloody spear fight or an all-night dance seemed somewhat less than an euphoric prospect.

It was a pleasant system. Alex liked the Kwosa. More importantly, the Kwosa liked the Kwosa. Unlike most peoples, they were enchanted with their way of life. They had no desire to change. In their view, it was madness to meddle with perfection.

Nomadic peoples have little in the way of bulky property. They are limited by what they can carry around with them. At first glance, the Kwosa had seemed unlikely prospects for the traders of Caravans.

However, they *did* have something. They had immense pride and vanity. They went in heavily for bodily adornment, and they were perfectionists.

As with many pastoral peoples, there was a special caste among the Kwosa. The caste was known as the Obo, and its members—male and female—were artisans. The Obo made the things that the Kwosa needed, the artifacts that the warriors had no time to produce. Basically, they were smiths. They smelted the iron for the essential spears. But the Obo made other things as well—leather straps and small iron pots and milking bags.

And jewelry.

Handcrafted jewelry for the most demanding customers in their sector of the universe.

Coils of fine wire, worn on arms and legs. Exquisite rings, necklaces, bangles for the ears. Feathered crowns crisscrossed with a delicate filigree of shining metal strands. . . .

It was the jewelry that Caravans wanted.

Jewelry designed for dancing warriors that almost sold itself on a crowded Earth that knew nothing but mass production.

And the jewelry was getting scarce.

Why?

The reasons was not complicated. The Kwosa had been hard-hit by raids. The hondari herds had been depleted. The people were not starving, but they were up against a dwindling food supply. They did not kill their precious hondari for meat, of course, but they depended upon them for their staple foods of milk and blood. (They made careful incisions in the hondari throats and drained off a cup of blood every few days.) Less food meant fewer Obo. Fewer Obo meant less jewelry.

Simple. It was a cyclical thing. The Kwosa were in no danger of extinction. In time, the balance would be restored.

But Caravans could not wait for generations. It had a waiting market. A few years, yes. A decade or two if necessary; they could take up the slack with other products.

They needed that jewelry, and the sooner the better.

Alex could handle the problem, or thought he could. (You could never be *sure* in this business.) But he needed freedom to act.

It was a lot tougher with Martin Ashtola looking over his shoulder. Alex had a double problem to solve. He had to restore the Obo production to its former level. And he had to convince Martin Ashtola that he was responding to the threat of the Others. . . .

Alex shook his head.

"Deliver me from Observers," he muttered.

He went to see Helen. She would understand. Understanding, she would make him forget.

For a while.

Tucker Olton held up the tube of bright red liquid that the lab boys had concocted. It looked very much like blood, except that the texture was too thin and the stuff lacked the darkness of true blood.

"Pretty, isn't it?" Alex Porvenir said with a sly grin.

"It looks like Exhibit A," Tucker Olton said. "In your sanity trial."

"Come now." Alex fired up his pipe, which was as foul-tasting as ever. "You've lost your faith in the old man."

"You really think you're going to palm this off on Ashtola?"

"I know I am. Getting it into the hides of the Kwosa will be the real trick."

"I'm not worried about that. Even as the junior partner in this team I think I could figure that one out. The Kwosa have this thing about bravery. They'll *love* shots just so they can show that pain doesn't bother them. That's why you're using syringes instead of some more modern method."

"That's one reason. The other is that we can teach the Kwosa to administer shots themselves. It doesn't take much in the way of special equipment or training."

"Okay, okay. But you can't sell Ashtola on this stuff. He isn't a complete "fool.""

"No, not a complete fool. He is, however, essentially a politician. He doesn't *know* anything."

"He knows there ain't no such animal."

"Does he? Want to bet?" Alex took the tube of red liquid from Tucker's hand. He held it up admiringly to the light. "Do *you* know what this is?"

"Not exactly, no. But I could—"

"I'll tell you what it is. It is Serum 247-B."

"Serum 247-B? What the hell is that?"

Alex puffed on his pipe. "You don't remember your history, Tuck. Serum 247-B was one of the last weapons created by the Biological Warfare Division of the Allied Armies in the Final War. It was never used. But all lightships carry a contingency supply for extreme emergencies."

"That's news to me, and I've been on a lightship with you for a lot of years. What does it do?"

"It subtly alters the endocrine system in such a way that it ultimately produces a psychologically superior fighting man. In short, a kind of superman. And it breeds true."

Tucker Olton stared at him. "You're telling me—"

67

"I assure you that it's the absolute truth."

Tucker Olton continued to stare at the older man. "Alters the endocrine system? How does that affect the genes?"

"It produces what might be termed a consistent and quite predictable mutation shift."

There was a long silence. Finally, Tucker Olton snorted—more in relief than anything else. "Alex, that is pure fantastic unadulterated fast-flowing crud. You know damned well it is."

Alex chewed on his pipe stem. "Serum 247-B. Had you going for just a minute there, didn't I?"

Tucker flushed. "I don't pretend to know everything. It's a defect of your teaching. It almost sounded reasonable at first."

Alex smiled. It was not a warm smile. "Look, friend. I know it's balderdash. You know it, because you're an intelligent man and have some scientific background. But Ashtola won't know it—not until it's much too late and we're light-years away from this place. If I can snow *you* a little I can bury *him* in an avalanche of fancy-sounding verbiage. It will work because he is what he is. He'll think it's just something he hasn't heard about, and he will *never* admit ignorance. It isn't his nature, believe me. He'll recognize good old Serum 247-B, despite the fact that it doesn't exist. He'll think the whole scheme is A Wonderful Plan. He may even try to get me a medal."

"That tube of red gunk won't solve our problem, though. It won't make more Obo."

Alex refilled his pipe and lit it. "Want to bet? You see, we're going to administer a slightly different version to the hondari herds too."

"Serum 247-C, I suppose?"

"How did you know? You probably don't remember, but in experiments some years ago at the Cuthbert Pomeroy Gundelfinger Institute of Veterinary Medicine they were able to prove beyond a shadow of a doubt—"

Tucker Olton threw up his hands. "Enough, already! I give up. Alex, you're going to be in some very hot water before this thing is over."

"I've been there before." Alex Porvenir looked at his associate with worried affection. "You may be in there with me, Tuck. That's why I think it is best if you don't know too much about what I'm really doing. For the present, I suggest you believe without reservation in the miraculous warrior-creating qualities of Serum 247-B."

"And Serum 247-C?"

"Certainly. Mighty warriors must have brave and ferocious hondari. Right?"

"Sure makes good sense to me."

Alex puffed on his pipe. "Trust me this once, Tuck. There's a lot at stake. Will you help me?"

Tucker Olton did not hesitate. "Of course," he said.

And that was that.

A child was born.

As the red sun beat down on the mud-and-dung plastered dome that was a Kwosa hut, a sweating woman crouched down and clutched her husband's spear that had been driven into the hard-packed dirt floor. It was the only occasion on which she could touch the spear of a man.

There was a small fire burning and it was very hot and smoky. There were no windows in the hut. There was one other person inside the structure, an old toothless woman who clucked knowingly and bustled about with an air of great importance.

Outside, unsheltered from the blazing sun, the men lounged around in little groups. They did not look at the hut. They gazed at the distant hondari herds. They talked about raids and the things that made the hondari beautiful. There was no way to tell which man was the woman's husband; his behavior was the same as all the others.

The swollen woman was in considerable pain. The child inside her was not coming easily. He was violent and kicking and stubborn. That was good.

He would be a boy.

Her face was contorted. The sweat poured from her body. She felt as though she were being torn apart.

She moaned a little. She did not cry out.

69

Her fingers contracted on the spear shaft until she thought she would splinter the wood. She tried to relax her grip. The spear must not be damaged.

The child emerged, slowly, encased in slime.

The old woman went into action. She was quick and efficient, despite her age. She had been through this many times.

In a matter of minutes the cord was cut and the sputtering infant was washed. Mother and child rested on the hide bed.

The old woman went to the door and gave a signal. The child's father detached himself from his group and entered the hut. He did not hurry. He kept his dignity. He tried to appear casual.

He permitted himself a brief smile when he saw that his child was a male. The Kwosa could use warriors.

He said nothing to his wife. That was the highest approval he could give.

He yanked the spear from the floor. Carefully, he placed it under the bed. The first day was important. The child could use all the help he could get.

He went back outside to study the remote hondari. He did not speak. In time, he would say what there was to say. In the meantime, the other men would not press him.

The Kwosa named their children on the fourth day. It was dangerous to give a name too soon. So many infants did not survive and it was best not to speak of them. That was easier when they had no name.

On the second day, two men from Caravans arrived at the hut. They stuck a needle into the baby's bottom and gave him an injection of bloodred fluid.

The baby whimpered a little but did not cry.

That was very good.

The father was proud of his son. He would give him a good name.

The Kwosa were not a people much given to group ceremonials. Dispersed and mobile as they were, there were few occasions when large numbers of people could get together for ritual observances.

There were a few important rites, however.

Like so many pastoral warrior societies, the Kwosa had an age-set system. As such organizations went, it was a fairly elaborate one. Each year, early in the summer when the grass was good and the herds could be bunched, all of the boys who had reached seventeen years of age were initiated into the warrior grade. At that time, they were circumcised and given their first man-sized spears. They were not yet full-fledged warriors, but they were no longer boys either.

Every four years all of the junior warriors—including those who had been circumcised that same year—moved up a notch, as did the groups senior to them. In time, a man served in all the warrior sets and advanced to the status of an elder.

The system was made to order for Alex Porvenir's plan— or perhaps it would be more correct to say that his plan was neatly designed to fit the system.

Caravans was in luck that the annual initiation was only three months away. Normally, even that span of time would have been much too long to wait; the logistics of interstellar trading made it mandatory to keep on the move. But the Kwosa were a crucial test case. Even though the Others had shown no interest in them as yet, the Others changed all the rules.

Caravans had to wait.

Martin Ashtola saw to that.

And wait they did—

Waited through the rains of spring, waited while the grass grew and the water filled the dry arroyos. . . .

Waited for boys to become men.

"It's barbaric," Martin Ashtola said.

"Yes," agreed Alex Porvenir.

"It gives me the creeps."

"Relax. *You* don't have to go through it." Alex Porvenir stuffed his pipe and lit it. He could feel his own blood racing to the pounding of the drums. "You wanted warriors. This is where you get them."

There were some thirty boys about to be initiated. There should have been nearly fifty.

They were trying hard not to look like boys. They were naked and their bodies were painted vertically with alternating white and crimson stripes. They stood straight, rigid, their hands at their sides. They did not move a muscle.

They faced two elders, one of whom held a hammer and a small chisel.

Beyond the two elders, a third man waited with an iron knife in his hand.

Behind the boys, the gathered Kwosa danced. The drums thudded and the rattles clacked. The warriors glittered with decorations as they leaped and twisted, showing off their beauty to the young women who moaned and grunted with ecstatic appreciation. The elders leaned on their spears and watched—and remembered.

Children stayed in their huts and watched from a distance. This was no place for children.

The red sun was low in the sky, but there was still plenty of light. There had to be.

The time had come.

The man with the iron knife lifted it toward the sun. The blade glinted dully.

The first boy stepped forward without hesitation. In a firm voice he announced his name and the name of his father. He walked to the two elders and lay down in the dirt, face up. He opened his mouth.

The elder with the hammer and chisel worked speedily. He wasted no motion. He knocked out an incisor tooth on the right side of the boy's lower jaw and then an incisor on the left side. Blood spurted from the boy's mouth. He swallowed what he could. He made no sound.

Sometimes, jaws were broken in that operation. It was never done on purpose, but it could be a good sign if the boy did not cry out. It was a test of character.

The second elder crouched down over the prostrate boy. He stuck a needle in the boy's left shoulder and rammed the plunger home. That was nothing.

"Serum 247-B?" whispered Martin Ashtola.

Alex nodded and puffed on his pipe. "Our little contribution to the ceremony," he said. "It will always be done now that the tradition is established."

The boy got to his feet. He swayed a little and spat out blood. He walked to the man with the knife. He lay down in the dirt again, face up. He spread his legs. He did not close his eyes.

The man cut him swiftly. There was considerably more blood.

The boy who was no longer a boy got to his feet. He had new crimson stripes now, on his chest and on his legs. He walked under his own steam back past the waiting boys. He did not look at them. In truth, he could hardly see.

His father came to him and covered his naked body with the cloak of a warrior. He pressed a heavy spear into his son's taut hand.

The new warrior marched with a nearly steady pace back to the hut where his mother was waiting.

Even warriors needed a mother sometimes, and this was emphatically one of the times.

The man with the bloody knife lifted it again toward the sun.

The second boy stepped forward.

"My God," said Martin Ashtola.

Alex Porvenir smiled grimly. "Only twenty-eight more to go," he said.

The drums continued to throb and the dancers strutted their stuff.

The elders nodded to one another, remembering many things. It was good to become a warrior.

The Caravans' lightship had left the system of Lalande far behind. It flashed through the gray wastes of nct-space.

Martin Ashtola had filed his first field report—which would not be received by the UN ET Council for many months after it was relayed from normal space—and he was quite well pleased with himself.

Alex Porvenir had filed a decidedly different report to Caravans. Carlos Coyanosa, the senior company representative on board, had already seen it. He was not happy about it. Alex was singularly unworried. Carlos was always upset by the actions that Alex took. He was a good man but he had no imagination.

Martin Ashtola did have a few nagging doubts.

"You're absolutely sure it will work?" he asked.

"Serum 247-B has never failed," Alex replied truthfully.

"Then we've really done something, haven't we? We're one up on them, and that's for sure."

"We've made us some warriors," Alex said. He was careful to speak the literal truth.

"It seems odd. I confess that I expected to see some sign of them on Lalande II."

"The Others?" Alex, one of the few men who had actually seen their traces on Arctica, found himself accepting the fact of their existence with composure.

"Of course. If we only knew more about what they were up to, how they thought! It's difficult operating in the dark, as it were. What are *their* plans for the Kwosa?"

Alex eyed the younger man. He looked quite natty in his clean blue uniform. *Ah, the thin blue line*, Alex thought. *Here he stands, one man alone, saving Earth from the slavering hordes.* "You have an awesome responsibility."

"It's funny we didn't run into them."

"Not really, Ash." Alex took a deep breath. He *had* to educate this man, however painful it was. He would wake up soon enough, and then the fur would fly. "It's only natural to expect to find *Them* everywhere, once we made the initial encounter. But it won't work that way. The universe is enormous, my friend, and the worlds in just our own little galaxy are beyond counting. We traders operated in space for a very long time before we even knew that *They* existed. It could be centuries before our paths cross again. They may not have any plans for the Kwosa at all."

"We can't act on that assumption! And even if we did, we've gained an advantage. We've made a move. We've done something for the Kwosa they couldn't do for themselves. We've turned them into magnificent warriors, and

74

Warning: The Surgeon General Has Determined That Cigarette Smoking Is Dangerous to Your Health.

Hello Max.

The maximum 120mm cigarette.

Great tobaccos. Terrific taste.
And a long, lean,
<u>all-white</u> dynamite look.

Menthol or Regular.

"Hello long, lean and delicious."

MENTHOL 120's by KENT

FILTER 120's by KENT

Regular: 17 mg. "tar," 1.3 mg. nicotine; Menthol: 18 mg. "tar," 1.3 mg. nicotine av. per cigarette by FTC Method.

Newport

Alive with pleasure!

Newport · 20 · CLASS A CIGARETTES · MENTHOL KINGS

7 mg. "tar", 1.2 mg. nicotine, av. per cigarette, FTC Report Apr. 75.

Warning: The Surgeon General Has Determined That Cigarette Smoking Is Dangerous to Your Health.

they'll be on *our* side when the showdown comes."

Hondari dung, Alex thought. "You think we did the right thing, then?"

"I'm certain of it. We have to act. We can't just sit back and wait."

"Yes, we must act. But there are actions and then there are actions. We are not gods, Ash. We have no private pipeline to the Ultimate Truth. We are entitled to make our own mistakes, and we've made plenty. But are we entitled to make decisions for other peoples?"

"You mean the Kwosa?"

"Among others, yes."

"Don't think I'm insensitive to the rights of native peoples! I'm here to protect them."

"Against the nasty old exploiting trading companies?"

"Well, I didn't mean that."

The hell you didn't.

"Look, Alex, I know your record—and that of Caravans. It's a very good one."

"Thank you."

"We did nothing to the Kwosa that they wouldn't want done. We know what's best for them. They *want* to be warriors."

"They also liked things the way they were. In fact, the Kwosa are among the few truly contented people I have ever known—and I have known a few."

"Serum 247-B won't *hurt* anyone."

"Perhaps not." Alex permitted himself a small smile. "I notice that you didn't volunteer to take any."

Martin Ashtola threw up his hands. He didn't understand this man at all. "That's totally different."

"Why?" Alex Porvenir asked quietly.

Martin Ashtola turned on his heel and left the room.

"Maybe you'd better explain," Tucker Olton suggested gently. "If I'm going to be in the line of fire, I'd like to know what in the hell I've been up to."

Alex Porvenir poured himself some Scotch and took a long

drink. He was tired and it was hard for him to look back. It was tough enough to make the decisions he had to make, year after year. It was tougher still to live with them afterward. He had no illusions about his own infallibility. He simply tried to do the best he could.

"Where do we start, Tuck? And please don't say at the beginning."

Tucker Olton shrugged. "As I see it, we had two basic problems with the Kwosa. Three, if you count Martin Ashtola. First, we were faced with a product loss because the Obo caste was declining in numbers and turning out less jewelry. Second, there was the long-range problem of the Others and how they might be countered or checked. Exactly what did we do?"

"We turned to good old Serum 247-B."

"Don't start *that* again."

Alex stiffened his drink and lit his pipe. The pipe was sour, as usual. He smoked it anyhow. The Scotch sweetened it some. "We might as well call it Serum 247-B. It sounds impressive and it's as good a name as any."

"Call it anything you like. What *is* it, and what does it do? Or is it just a smokescreen for Ashtola?"

"Pretty good pun there. Congratulations. You're learning."

"Please, Alex."

"Okay. Sorry. The red gunk we used in the shots is chemically complex but medically simple. It consists of inoculations against basic childhood and adult diseases, periodic-releasing antibiotics, and long-term vitamins. That's all. It will not protect against every known disease, of course, but it will hit the most common Kwosa ailments. It will also help in recovering from wounds, including infections from a dirty circumcision knife."

"No super warriors?"

"Nope. It won't do a thing in that direction. It will not change the Kwosa one damned bit."

"How does that solve our product problem?"

"You're not thinking, Tuck. It won't create any super

76

warriors but it will result in *more* warriors—and more Kwosa generally. We did essentially the same thing with the hondari herds. More Kwosa, more Obo. More Obo, more jewelry. We'll get our product back.''

Tucker Olton nodded slowly. ''I hadn't thought of attacking it from that angle.''

Alex took a long swallow from his drink. He was feeling a shade better. ''Our basic problem with the Kwosa was population decline. It was caused by raiding, as you know—a loss of hondari and a loss of fighting men. The cycle would adjust itself in time, but we speeded it up a little. Instead of providing the Kwosa with new defensive tactics or new weapons, we cut down on infant mortality and increased the survival rate from combat wounds. We also reduced hondari losses from natural causes, thereby increasing the herds. The Kwosa will do fine. They'll be there long after you and I are dead and gone.''

''And the Others? Do we just forget about them?''

''No. That would be a fatal mistake.''

''But we left the Kwosa just as we found them.''

''I think that's precisely the point.''

''I'm afraid I don't quite follow that.''

Alex cleaned out his pipe, after a fashion, and tamped in another load. He lit it evenly for a change and blew out a small cloud of smoke. ''Look, Tuck. What do we *know* about the Others, leaving aside all the hysterical blather? We know that they represent an alien civilization, the only one besides our own that seems to be operating in space at the present time. We know that they tried to *change* the Lupani on Arctica—change them in a way that was not in the best interests of the Lupani themselves. That's all we have to go on. Presumably, they are trying to change other cultures elsewhere. It makes sense to assume that they have a plan of some sort; they're not doing it just for the hell of it. The plan involves altering cultures according to some kind of a master design.''

''I'll buy that. There's no argument. And so?''

''And so our course of action is plain enough even for us to see—and we will come to see it eventually. We may be stupid occasionally, or even frequently, but we are not stupid *all* the time.''

"I must be in my stupid phase. I don't see any howlingly obvious solution.''

"Try this one, by way of an interim policy. We know they want to *change* things—change them by interference, not by way of natural development. Okay. If we come across their work, as we did on Arctica, we try to undo it. We *restore* the original culture, unless there is some compelling reason for not doing so. That counters their plan, whatever it is. If we deal with untouched lifeways, as we usually do, we *don't* change them except in very minor ways. We leave them as they are and trade with them as we always have.''

"Business as usual?''

Alex sipped his drink. "We have to keep Caravans and the other trading companies afloat. They are our eyes in space, our only way of knowing what goes on in our own universe. What we *don't* do is to go off half-cocked on some nutty scheme of galactic tinkering—at least not until we know almost infinitely more than we do now.''

"You'll never sell Ashtola on that. He wants action.''

"He's human. He can learn. There are a lot of of people like Martin Ashtola who are going to have to think this thing through to a sane conclusion. They'll get there, given enough time. They'll get there, or Earth isn't worth bothering about. I hate to mention it, but there *are* ethical considerations involved. And morality has a way of being practical, sometimes.''

"I wish you'd spell that out.''

"I intend to. You'll get sick of hearing it—and so will a lot of other people before I'm through. Let's go back to the analogy of colonialism.''

"Again?''

"One more time. It's an instructive example. On Earth, back in the bad old days, colonialism occurred when there was a radical power imbalance between political and geographical units. The technologically superior units moved in and took over the administration of the so-called undeveloped units. Because they *were* so powerful—relatively—they believed that they were intellectually and morally superior as well. They justified their actions with some very noble-sounding philosophies.''

"I've heard all that before, Alex.''

"Maybe you haven't heard this. The colonial powers weren't devils. They were not guilty of all the diabolical evils attributed to them. If it hadn't been for colonialism, some of our friends sitting in judgment today on the UN ET Council wouldn't be there. The wicked colonialists generally did the best they could, given the times and the attitudes and the usual fallibility of human beings. But they *were* guilty of one monstrous crime. And that, oddly enough, was paternalism. It was the doctrine of Father Knows Best—and its inevitable corollary, Other People Are Children.''

"I think I see where you're going.''

"Yes.'' Alex puffed on his pipe. "Either we learn from the past or we are nothing. That's the one mistake we cannot afford to make in space. Paternalism. It's so easy for us to fall into the habit of thinking that *we* should make basic decisions about the lifeways of other peoples who are not in a position to know what is going on. I tell you, we *don't* know everything—not with all our sciences and computers and technology. Neither do the Others, whoever or whatever they are.''

"Do we just plead ignorance, then? If it is wrong to use other peoples as pawns, what happens if we become pawns ourselves?''

Alex drained his final drink. "We won't. We're not just sitting on our ethical butts as long as Caravans continues to function. We can undo what the Others do. We can help people by permitting them to go their own way. The true confrontation is centuries in the future. If we conduct ourselves properly and do the best we can, we will end up with partners rather than pawns. Which would you rather have when the chips are down? You know, the Kwosa is a pretty damned good fighting man just as he is.''

"I hope you're right, Alex.''

Alex Porvenir nodded. The old doubts crept into his mind

again. "That makes two of us," he said slowly. "That makes two of us."

Later, Alex turned to Helen and touched her shoulder.

"Do I look like a crazy old man to you?" he asked.

"I can't see you."

"You can remember."

Helen kissed him sleepily. "A little crazy, dear. A little old. Definitely a man. You'll do, love. Don't worry. Go to sleep."

Alex closed his eyes.

Later still, the Caravans lightship emerged from the grayness of not-space.

The universe took her in, absorbed her—a universe of vastness and color and life.

Against the scale of space, the little ship with its incongruous symbol of a laden camel was nothing. It was less than a grain of sand in the desert.

And yet it counted for something, that ship. It counted because of what it was and what it carried.

Fears, hopes, dreams—

Imperfections and a spark of something better—

Yes.

In a wilderness of stars, it would do.

It made a difference.

Thomas N. Scortia

THE ARMAGEDDON
TAPES—TAPE IV

FOR the history of mankind before the Fusion was one of cruelty and a willingness to spill the blood of millions for some abstract ideal. There were definitions of "good" and of "evil" in their philosophy just as, in a fashion, there were such concepts in the total racial consciousness of the antlike Angae. The Fusion of human and Angae consciousness into the superconsciousness was Martin's prime objective and to this end he saw no contradiction in forcing the bloody destruction of a quarter of his own race. A poet of the period wrote: "that we teach bloody destruction that returns to plague the hand of the inventor. . . ." (A very free translation.) It was appropriate that in the end, with the ever looming menace of the Theos encroaching on this galaxy, that trifling distinctions of good and evil ceased to trouble the thoughts of the Messiah and of his opponents. . . .

—*Die Anelan De Gakactea*, Vol. II, Ca. 3400

IN the midst of personal disaster, there came to me the highest honor I had ever hoped of achieving as an Inquisitor. (Yes, of course, the time sequences become confused but it has to be put down in this manner. One alters one's viewpoint, returns to the beginnings. . . .)

On that day his Exalted Plurality, the Anointed Premier of our Holy State himself, came to me at my home in Cherry Chase. I had spent the weekend resting and thinking back over the events of the past year. For once the daily raids of the alien ships on the outlying cities had not come and the weekend had been undisturbed although several times hungry people clustered around my doorstep. They could see the signs of wealth in my household . . . the lights at night, the bread crusts in the garbage can, the intact windows on the second floor. (They did not realize that the second floor had already been stripped for wood for the fireplace because the central gas supply had been exhausted.) They clustered around my front stoop, begging for food, until I had the two deacons who attended me drive them away. One Citizen, I am told, was seriously injured but I could not be bothered. The Holy State would take care of his wounds and, if they were serious, he would find his way to the Fields.

I was resting since I became very fatigued in those days, though I was only thirty-five. You would not have believed this since I had the look of a man of sixty, but it was true. That beast, the anti-State, who bore the most banal name of Martin, had taken my youth and vigor from me in that terrible night in southern Illinois, and it had not returned. Age and fatigue or not, I swore I would have him yet. If only I had the full power to marshall all of our dwindling resources to track him down, I knew I might yet save our Holy State from his depredations. He had made common cause with the sickening insect creatures whose captive he once was, and they ranged over our sacred Earth, despoiling the cities and slowly eroding the power of the Holy State. It was truly Armageddon and I sat there, a young man in an old man's body, frustrated at my inability to meet the threat, to find my own terrible personal revenge on the Great Beast.

But no longer.

His Exalted Plurality came to me that day. There was a great flurry outside the door as his armored fleets turned into the street and came to the circular cul-de-sac where my house stood. I heard the chatter of micro-Brens, driving away the straggling citizens, and the loud blare of warning trumpets and the heavy pound of armored fists on my door. One of my deacons scurried to answer and then hurried back, his eyes wide and fearful, for who of the common herd before has ever gazed upon the Anointed Premier in the flesh and lived? It was a sign of the desperate state of our affairs that it should have been so now.

His archdeacons, fierce in their armor, entered the room without knocking and ignored me as they searched the area, going out on the patio where they met other deacons, investigating the grounds behind the house. As soon as they were sure of the security of the area, they ranged themselves silently on either side of the door and I heard the heavy footsteps of his coming. I was reclining on the chaise longue with a quilt over my legs as he entered the study. When I tried to rise, he signaled for me to remain seated, a remarkable sign of the greatness of the man.

I insisted on rising, however, and I made the proper ceremonial gesture of obedience and fealty. "Enough of this, Inquisitor Jarvis," he said impatiently and turned to mutter something to the handsomely garbed man at his elbow. I was surprised to see that it was the Anointed Majority leader and for a moment a quaking fear seized me. I cursed the old body I wore, for a year ago I would have swollen with pride at the honors coming to me.

I heard the Premier mutter, "Well, if you're sure. I'm not impressed, but if you're sure. . . ." The Majority Leader whispered in turn and the Premier turned to me.

"We have little time for ceremony these days, Inquisitor, with our Holy State menaced on every side."

"I know this better than any citizen, your Plurality," I said.

"So I am told," he said with a scowl. I had a moment to see him clearly. He was a magnificent figure of a man, tall, lean and ascetic-looking with a high widow's peak and fierce eyes. There was an aura of power and dedication about him that seemed to sweep you into his orbit and evoked simultaneously a fear and a comfort.

(That's not true, of course. He was a very ordinary-looking man, tall with a heavy middle and sagging folds under his eyes. His nose was laced with blue veining that suggested too much indulgence in food and drink and he spoke with a distinct hoarseness, mumbling his words so that you had to listen very closely to understand him.)

(No, that wasn't the way I saw him.)

(That was the way he *was*. Your conception was produced by the Mettler serum coupled with your lifelong conditioning. You could not have seen him otherwise. Why do you think the Holy State came into being and persisted as long as it did?)

"I am persuaded," the Premier said dourly, "that you know more of this . . . this Great Beast that menaces us than anyone else in the State. Is this true?"

"Yes," I said. "I have followed him since the early days when he and his companions who were captives aboard the alien ship forced it down in the Carolina Smokies. I have watched his slow evolution from a mere child called Martin into the destroying menace that he is today."

The Premier found a seat and sighed wearily. "Is he human? Above all else, is he human?"

"Yes, he is certainly human, but far more than human," I said. I told him of how Martin and the other children . . . the ones I had fortunately destroyed in the Carolinas . . . had been spirited away from the State by their parents, how they had been secluded in the barren north countries because of their special talents that would have been used or erased by the State. How the alien ship came down and captured them, how the aliens changed their biochemistry so that for a while they were part of that strange ship society, functioning as "cows" (to use Martin's term) in a sort of ant-aphid symbiosis. They had, through their special talents, learned much from the nameless aliens and in due course, after their parents had died in captivity, they were able to immobilize the aliens, and force the ship to land in the Smokies. There they seized Cherokee, the Indian village that held the last of the tribes, the ones whose biochemistry was so resistant to the Mettler serum that we had cast them from the body of the Holy State.

I told him of the attack of the Faithful upon the ship, the capture of Martin and his subsequent escape after destroying the mind of the Interrogator who had questioned him. I told him of my interrogation of the captured Cherokee, John Talltrees, who had briefly offered Martin friendship and who had brought him from the disgusting cannibalism, that allowed them to preserve the personalities of their dead fellows, to the ceremony of blood-sharing that now bound his peoples together.

"I wish you could have destroyed him with the other children," the Premier said fervently.

"Thank the State that there is only one to contend with, though their essences still exist in him and his followers."

"Traitors," the Majority Leader swore.

"No," I said, "something far more deadly. He assimilates them, the very personalities of his followers. My science advisors have told me that it is much like a continuous preservation of the very structure of personality, that the nuclei acid pattern of each follower is endlessly duplicated through the whole body of his people. That is his strength, their belief that they cannot die.

"When the aliens, who had fled some disaster that destroyed their world, changed their plans and remained here in an attempt to destroy him, it was this which he had learned from them that gave him strength. This, and his knowledge of their insight into the fine phenomena of the universe, that gave him the special powers that baffle us now. When he found the woman, the Black named Vera, I almost had him. At the very moment when he finally made contact with the aliens in southern Illinois and they made common cause, I was close to destroying him. Only he came upon me unguarded, and did what you see now."

"What happened to you?" the Premier demanded.

I shuddered, as the memory came back vividly. "He took my blood," I said.

"Blood-sharing?"

"No, he took my blood and in a moment I had aged to what I am now. For this I would hunt him with the last breath of my life and destroy him."

He looked at me, frowning. My anger had invaded my voice and the last words sounded almost hysterical. I leaned forward fiercely. He smiled a dry smile. "So be it," he said. "I am convinced. Inquisitor, the State is at an end unless we may finally destroy the Beast. I think you can do this. The full resources of the State will be yours to meet him and destroy him. This is the commission I want to give you. Will you accept?"

For a moment I was overwhelmed. I had never dreamed of such an honor. Then a sense of wild triumph came to me, a soaring savagery that I had not felt in a year. At last, I would have the power to bring him groveling, to wrack his body and scatter it to the Holy Fields. I would put an end to him at last.

"Accept?" I asked. "I could not do anything else."

"Good," the Anointed Premier said and rose. He left without a word. The Majority Leader stayed behind to give me instructions and to introduce me to a small saturnine man named Fleming who was to be my assistant and adjutant in this great undertaking. Fiercely I promised myself that I would destroy this creature who had wrecked my life and my State. I found my thoughts almost drowned in the continuing silent chant of "at last, at last, at last."

We established our command post in the ruined basement of St. Blair house, tunneling down into the earth to create three layers of concrete subbasements. This was necessary since we could not be sure that the incursions of the alien ships would not eventually include the capital itself. The aliens had been highly selective in their attacks, primarily because their ships were limited in number and our rocket pursuits were often their equal within the atmosphere. Lately they seemed only to attack military groupings that menaced communities in which Martin had been. That Beast was like some Black Messiah moving across the land, and where he went, there remained a mass of citizens committed to him. They believed his doctrine of unity utterly and they swore that he wanted only to weld humanity and the aliens into one great whole to meet an unnamed menace that was moving across the galaxy toward us. It was a fantastic doctrine and they believed it utterly because in accepting him, they became literally a part of him.

The centers of the infection circled the globe, small towns and the tattered remains of the great cities. He had been in each of them or someone who resembled him and had his powers. The source of these powers were beyond me. I had been told that somehow he perceived the fine structure of the universe, that he could manipulate forces that we had not even defined. This he and the other children had learned from the aliens although they had amplified on the talents of the aliens whose use of these powers was localized and limited. Wherever he went, he fed the people and clothed them and comforted them, turning them from our Holy State. He brought them the obscene ritual of sharing blood and they became one with him. After that they were irrevocably lost to us.

"So be it," I told my aide, Fleming. "We cannot recover them, but the State has always had its recalcitrants. These are the ones we sent to the Holy Fields and if we have to send half the population of the continent, even of the Holy Earth itself to the Fields, we will root out this infection and eventually we will find its source and destroy it."

"I admire your fervor," he said somewhat disdainfully. "How are you prepared to carry this out though?"

"With a ruthlessness you cannot imagine," I said.

"I can imagine ruthlessness," he said. "I wonder if you are capable of it."

"That's easily enough demonstrated," I told him and began to prepare the plans for the great sweep. "If an infected limb cannot be cured," I told Fleming, "we cut it off. I will cut off every infected member of the State that we cannot cure to control this disease. In the end we will have the Holy State returned to its health. A generation will heal our wounds just as another generation healed the wounds of the Great Disaster that almost destroyed human society."

"Sometimes I wonder at your sanity," he said.

I felt a surge of anger at this. I had already grown to dislike this small dark man with a special dislike, and I had promised myself some special attention to him when the emergency was over. For the moment I needed him. "Sanity is unimportant at the moment," I told him. "Only the destruction of the Beast and his converts matters."

"To be sure," he said, retreating before the force of my argument. I could see the worry and the fear in his eyes, but he continued to obey me. Even he feared the Fields.

There was precedent enough for what we did, although not on such a grand scale. There was Nero and his Christian torches that lighted his gardens. The endless massacres for one faith or another through the long bloody history of the race. Ivan the Terrible, a despot of pre-Disaster Europe slaughtered tens of thousands of his citizens before the Great Gates of Kiev. Indeed, he tortured them and flayed them and brought them bleeding to their graves, blessing him and confessing to him, all in the name of that God that we rejected for the Holy State long ago. He did all this and remained in power, feared and beloved by his citizens. With the complete conditioning of our population through the Mettler serum, how much more might we now dare and still preserve the structure of the Holy State?

(This was a nightmare, a sign of the fundamental weakness of the species.)

(Truly? Here we disagree, for the response is built into the race. When faced with such odds and such menace, death and blood have always been the answer. Will you use some such obsolete term as "evil" to describe what we did?)

(No, we've been through all that before. The definitions of "good" and "evil". . . . What do they mean in the long history of a race? "Pain" perhaps has meaning. Death certainly does not. Good and evil, mere sides of a coin.)

We marshalled our archdeacons and our deacons and we sent them out to the focal points of the infection. To Chicago and to Rome where I had before that last disastrous confrontation with the Beast. To southern Illinois where last we had met. We proposed to consolidate the parts of the globe by starting at the points of earliest infection and working outward. This meant a fantastic exercise in logistics. We had to commandeer every bit of transport, even at the risk of bringing famine to the provinces of the State. We had to marshall and move whole divisions of men and their equipment. We had to feed them and clothe them and quarter them while they were engaged in their Holy Work. More, we had to monitor their work and control them from this central point. The communication equipment that went into our headquarters alone would have sufficed for the needs of two provinces.

And consider the weaponry and the logistics for transporting those we found to be infected to the Holy Fields. The logistics were staggering. It is not easy to plan the death and dissolution of hundreds of thousands of citizens, even millions. The strain on the economy and on the organization of the State, still recovering from the Great Disaster and now reeling under the military attacks of the aliens, was fantastic. With a large and devoted staff, with the almost single-minded devotion of Fleming (he did have virtues), we began the task.

In the first week in Chicago, we consigned ten thousand citizens to the Fields. Every hundreth we interrogated, but for the most part we assumed guilt by association. If they were a part of the community the Beast had visited, they were infected. We plucked them out.

In Rome where the infection was more deep-seated, nearly twenty-five thousand were lost to the State. Here the logistics problem broke down for the transportation system of southern Europe is notoriously undependable. Yet, our Faithful did not let that deter them in their holy mission. I arranged for supplies of cholera and typhoid vaccine to be sent to the area when it became apparent that the huge numbers who could not be consigned to the Fields had in their corruption become a hazard to the health of the Faithful.

In Tokyo, in all of the Indian subcontinent, in Australia, in southern California the Holy Work went on. The citizens bowed before our Faithful like wheat before the blade of the harvester. Many, I'm sure, were not infected by the Beast. I mourned for these, but consoled myself with the thought that in such drastic surgery, healthy tissue must be excised to assure that all of the contaminated flesh is destroyed.

I was winning against the Beast. I knew it and I exulted at the pain that I must be causing him. I sat in the evening in the depths of my quarters and read and reread the reports, savoring the coming fruits of victory over this creature who had plagued me and who had stolen so much from me. The numbers delighted me, excited me sometimes to a frenzy of ecstasy when I realized that to me had come that one great moment in history denied to so many men. I and I alone would save the Holy State.

At the end of the first week of the work, the Premier came to me in my quarters. His face was drawn and there was a look in his eyes that I had seen increasingly in the eyes of the men about me. It was a look I could not define, but it troubled me for they should have been sharing in my elation at the sight of victory. The Premier said, "My God, man, what are you doing?"

"God?" I asked. "Surely, your Plurality, you don't mean such an exclamation. There is no God, only the Holy State."

"You are slaughtering my citizens," he said.

"It is the only way," I said. "We must meet the menace with the same ruthlessness with which it attacks us."

"But so many?" He sank to an ottoman, his body sagging as though he were as fatigued as I. Still, I reminded myself, he did not have the grand vision to sustain himself in his fatigue as I did. I began slowly and patiently to explain to him why it was necessary. I painted him a picture of the horror that would result if we did not do this. The alternative was enough to chill even his spirit and finally he rose and agreed that this was the way it must be. Before he left, he ordered me to spare him the detailed reports I had been sending him.

"I don't want to know about it," he said. "I only want to know what areas are secure."

He left and in spite of myself I smiled. So, he was, after all, only a man. My loyalty to him was undimmed, but I saw that he had the fault of so many men whose inner weakness prevented them from acting rigidly according to their principles. He wanted to be ignorant of the details and I promised myself that he would. Perhaps he needed this lack of knowledge to escape some inner feeling of responsibility. I could not understand this emotionally, but intellectually it made sense. I, therefore, instructed my staff to send him only highly edited and completely impersonal reports.

The Work went on.

They no longer came willingly to our interrogations. No longer did they stand as we cut them out, goats from sheep. They gathered together in the inner cities or in the open fields. This happened in Boston, in Vienna, in Karachi. It became necessary to resort at times to other means. Actually, they made it a great deal more convenient for us. Instead of excising each individual cell, we now had whole tissues clustered in one spot. A quick touch of the surgical knife and the work was done. Our supplies of the Forbidden Weapons were limited, but I felt sure the bombs we had were equal to our Holy Task.

This phase of the Work went on for three days before a change in tactics was reported to me. In the meantime I had become troubled with stories of defections among our Faithful. It seemed impossible in people conditioned from the cradle for the service of the Holy State, but defections there were. Whole platoons and then whole companies. It became necessary to turn some of our Holy Fire upon those that should have been ours. Another man would have hesitated at this but I did not.

Even Fleming protested. I warned him of the dangerous ground upon which he stood. I gave the order. He obeyed. When he protested that the attrition was too great, I told him, "By the Holy State, I will bring every man and woman and child on the Holy Earth, saving only those last in this city, to the Fields if this is the only way to rid us of this menace. It is the only solution and under the charge of the Anointed Premier himself I will have this solution . . . finally and irrevocably." Then I gave him the order and he left to obey. I marked him in my private book. In the end he too would answer for interfering with my inspired task.

Blighted little mouse of a man; I had thought him strong. Yet, he was afraid to bring me news at first of the shift in tactics. I heard of the Beast's continued activities, moving across the land with his message and bringing new pockets of infection, but Fleming hesitated to tell me how the Beast now countered our grand surgery. It was only after the third day, when the statistics of those who had been excised began to drop alarmingly, that I brought him before me and demanded an explanation.

He told me then of the death of the Premier that morning. I could not believe that he would die by his own hand, but he had very simply done so. I wondered that he had kept poison so close at hand. The thought came to me that perhaps he had not been as thoroughly conditioned as a loyal citizen should be. It may well be, I thought, that the same low level of conditioning applied to the others of the Anointed Diet, to even the Majority Leader himself. How, I wondered, could such men rise to the seat of power? They would bear watching and, if need be, in the service of the Holy State I would bring any of them to the Fields. No man is greater than the State, not even those that the State has chosen to anoint.

"Why has he done this?" I demanded.

Fleming would not speak at first but I pressed my demands. Reluctantly at last he told me that he had been sending the statistics to the Premier in spite of his refusal to look at them.

"That was a direct disobedience of his orders. Why did you continue to do so?"

"He did not look at them," Fleming said. "He refused to look at them."

"But why did you continue to send them?"

"He was the head of the Holy State. He could not escape the responsibility for what was done in Its Name and in his."

"Your reasoning is seriously in error," I said. "The State assumes Its own responsibility. We are its servants only."

"The State does not exist as a separate entity," he argued. "The State is not God."

"Of course not. There is no God. Only the Holy State and it exists as a composite being in space and time. The State is timeless and perfect. It will endure."

He made the ritual motions, but I could see that he was troubled and that the shadow of doubt lurked in his eyes. I marked that for future action. Now, I could not spare him, any more than I could spare any of the legions of men that now invested my headquarters.

"There is more," I accused. "This much you have kept from me and I suspect a great deal more."

"No, no, nothing," he said. I could see that he was lying.

"The statistics are lower than I expected. Are we that close to success?" I could hardly keep the scorn from my voice. He was clearly afraid and the fear brought a tremor to his hands so that the papers he clutched rattled like dry straw. Was it fear of me? He had reason enough to fear me now, but then I saw that it was a greater fear even than that.

"Tell me," I demanded. "What have you been keeping from me?"

I could have killed him on the spot, my fury was so complete. Only my better sense prevailed, my realization that I could not discard this defective tool at this point simply because there was not another. Better the defective tool for whose defects you can compensate than no tool at all. Still, my anger reached proportions that I would not have thought possible. I had grown accustomed to my blighted body and the low emotional fires in it. I did not believe that such rage could seize me.

(Since when is rage a prerogative of youth?)

(The ability to express that rage is. That is why youth is so deadly.)

(Since when have the old men of the world been so peaceful? Who in our history has sent the young men to die in their causes?)

(Yes, but that was not rage; that was merely politics.)

Trembling he told me what had happened in the last few days. The story was completely unbelievable. Yet, after these years of contending with the Beast, I knew that he was capable of even this madness. To turn a whole race into savages, to loose them upon their fellows and upon the Holy State itself. Yes, in spite of my first doubts, there was no question in my mind that he could do it, that he was in fact doing it.

They had marshalled themselves passively in the cities and in the fields and we had swept the Forbidden Fire over them. Only now they were no longer passive. From the great focal points, particularly from Chicago, they were moving out.

Imagine a mass of people, a great carpet of humanity moving across the land. Like some swarm of locusts or . . . more appropriately . . . like a mass of army ants, ceaselessly on the move, cutting a swath through the countryside.

Not aimlessly. They were moving east, always east, their numbers swollen by other cities, by villages, by hamlets. All of these had been incorporated into the vast mass intelligence that the Beast had created. They overwhelmed our ground troops, the Faithful upon which I had counted, and the Faithful became one with them.

I drove Fleming from my presence, then called him back. Fleming was frightened, completely cowed. I gave him orders that our aircraft were to attack the columns. Destroy them if possible, but certainly contain them until the inevitable famine would come upon them. How does one feed a restless multitude, numbering in the millions, as they move across the land? In a concentrated form they presented a logistic problem that cannot be solved. They would begin to starve, I knew. They would drop and die and this final great gamble of the Beast would fail.

Fleming left to give the orders. Now, I realize that I should have been surprised that they were obeyed. The dissolution of our Holy State had proceeded that far. Still, they obeyed, these last of the Faithful, but before they could do more than mount the first attacks, the ships of the aliens came down upon them in such fury that they could not defend themselves. We lost five pursuits in the Illinois area, fell back to regroup the combined forces and attacked again. The aliens met us and, though they lost three ships themselves, they drove us back.

The last attack was over Detroit and the pitiful remains of our continental fleet were no match for them. I marked the passing of the Faithful pilots in my day journal and looked to the east, to Europe and Asia. The same thing was happening there. Already our fleets were decimated to the point that I saw there was no use in further contention. Nevertheless, I ordered them to the attack and they obeyed. They obeyed and slowly but certainly they died until at last Fleming brought the word that there were none left. The great moving hordes were unopposed.

"Never mind," I said. "No one in history has ever moved such an army, much less a mass of unprepared rabble. They will starve and we will be burying their bones for a century."

But they came on. They did not starve. The swollen river of humanity passed east, entered upper New York and turned south. Not one dropped of exhaustion, not one died of hunger. The few reconnaissance jets left to me brought the pictures and I saw the incredible sight laid out before me.

I had likened them to a vast wave of Army ants, but the ants live off forage from the land. They strip every plant bare as they move, but humans cannot live on grass and reeds and trees. Until now.

Like cows, they ate every bit of vegetation in sight. I remembered then that the aliens had changed Martin and the children, altered their biochemistry to handle cellulose and that later he and the children had done this to members of the village in the Carolinas. How he did this on such masses of people I do not know, but I realized that they had solved their logistics problem. The path they took lay across the most forrested lands and the grassiest plains of the continent. And they had not starved.

Imagine this final destiny for humanity, to be reduced to a carpet of identityless beings, to move like one blind animal across the land, stripping it of its vegetation. A nightmare horror that was suddenly reality.

Blind, did I say? No, they were not blind. They were clearly coming upon us here in the Holy City. In days they had traversed the distance and the last of the Faithful were pressed back inevitably, finally to the limits of the Holy City itself. We sat in the depths of this last citadel of ours and heard the reports of the gathering flood at our gates. The people of the coasts had swollen the tide and now there was no stopping it. In a matter of weeks we had become besieged by a mass of humanity, the like of which the world had never seen. The Faithful in our citadel faded away and at long last Fleming came to me.

His eyes were haunted with fear. He carried a small case with him. I sat at my desk, reading the last of the reports when he came in. "It's all over," he said.

"Yes," I said. "It seems impossible, but it is all over."

"The Holy State is dead," he said.

"No," I said. "Not while I am alive."

"Don't you realize what they will do?" he asked.

"No, no, not what you think," I said. "I know this Black Beast far better than you."

"I brought you this," he said and opened the small case. There was a single pellet of potassium cyanide resting inside.

I smiled bitterly and said, "No, that was the way for the faithless Premier and his sychophants. It is not the way for me."

"Then I will leave," he said.

"Is this what you plan," I asked.

"Yes," he said wearily.

"Then do it now. Do it here."

He stared at me in disbelief. "Here, in front of you?"

"It is my wish and I am the Holy State."

He started to object, but the conditioning was still too strong within him. He took the pellet from the case and, as I watched, he swallowed it. I watched as he felt the first searing touch of the alkaline salt in his stomach, watched the sudden gasping for breath, the livid blue that crossed his features. He collapsed, falling forward into my arms. I looked down at his contorted face and thought how sorry I was that I had not been able to take him to the Fields in one of the many ways I knew. It would have been a small luxury in the end.

I sat and waited and I heard the mutterings outside even through the concrete and the earth piled above me. I knew they would not enter. They would wait for him and in the end he would come. In something less than an hour, I heard his footsteps echoing down the hollow corridors outside. I wondered if the woman would be with him. I hoped not for I remembered her in quite a different context. The State was good. He came alone.

"I knew you were too strong to do that," he said, gesturing at Fleming's sprawled form. He had grown since I last saw him. He was older and his face now held a distant look as though it shifted form constantly with the warring entities that were a part of him. He was Martin as I once knew him and he was not Martin, he was a thousand, a million beings . . . All-man.

"I could not kill myself," I said. "I am the Holy State."

"Consistent to the end," he said.

"What else is there in life?" I demanded.

"This," he said. He thrust forth his hand and the wrist opened as if with a knife. The brightest arterial blood sprang forth. "I took your essence once but denied you mine. It is now time."

"No," I said, but I felt his strength flow across to me and I had no choice. I realized that there was something within me, forcing me. It was the essence, as he called it, the blood he had once stolen from me. There was no choice. I drank and the wound closed and. . . .

(And I am one with you, one with this great man-beast that you have made of the peoples of the world.)

(Are you?)

(I feel the multitudes sprawling in my mind.)

(But you are not one with us, not assimilated.)

(Is it so? Is it truly so, that I have not joined this consummate evil even now?)

(What is evil? We talked earlier of that.)

(Earlier? Now? Confused.)

(The time sense becomes confused. All that happened years ago.)

(And evil, of course, evil. What else?)

(To be rejected. Have you ever considered that evil is the template of good and the reverse? Like the DNA, the nucleic acid, that was the basis for your serum and for the survival of your personality now. It has a template, messenger ribonucleic acid. The messenger RNA is the template for the body's synthesis of the DNA and vice versa. One implies the other. Good implies evil and evil implies good. One has no meaning without the other.)

(And you? What role will you assign yourself?)

(It's of no matter now. You behaved as I expected you to,

as I forced you to. I was your template, so to speak.)

(You controlled me?)

(Was there ever any doubt? After I had taken your essence, there was no doubt.)

(To meet some great imagined menace, you did all this? What menace?)

(It is enough that I know it exists. I had to be the final judge. Because there were those I could not control. Because there was so little time to meet the coming Menace that I see through the eyes of aliens.)

(You slaughtered a million souls for this, just to save time?)

(It was expedient.)

(He has withdrawn for the moment along with the others. It seems I remain unique, never completely assimilated. While I have exclusive control of this now young-again body, I can talk. To whom? It doesn't matter. Just to get the words on tape.)

(I don't understand. Surely there must be a difference. There had to be a difference or there was no point to what I did. I wanted to save the State and yet, he tells me, I did exactly what he told me to do.)

(I look down at the dead body of poor Fleming, Fleming who cannot live again because of the cyanide that fills his body. That is the one physical thing we cannot or will not . . . I don't know which . . . assimilate. I look down at him and remember that there was another Fleming, ages and ages ago. What did he do? Invented a new drug I think, a drug that cured so many diseases. Penicillin, I think.)

(Only after years of use, the drug became useless. The infections became immune to the drug and in the end they actually fed upon it.)

(Ironic. A fitting name for him.)

(Shall I now feed upon myself?)

Anne McCaffrey

KILLASHANDRA—CODA
AND FINALE

"SO the galaxy stands in dire need of more blue orthorhombics," said Killashandra with savage glee. "Sorry. Lanzecki. The gyros on my flitter have had it. It'd be suicide to go before they've been changed and tuned, and you know how long that takes. Right now, I've enough credit to take me off this barfing world for a good long time. And I'm going!"

She'd turned to go but Lanzecki's voice, never before so uncompromisingly authoritarian, and as emotionless as if his precious computer had developed a voice, stopped her midstride.

"No, Killashandra Ree, you are not going."

Slowly, because she didn't believe her ears, Killashandra turned back to Lanzecki.

"I'm not going?" Her voice was too quiet. Someone else, knowing Killashandra as long as Lanzecki had, would have demurred or made some attempt to placate her imminent anger.

Instead, Lanzecki's fingers flew across the computer console, though his eyes never left hers. Involuntarily Killashandra looked up at the computer printout panel behind the Guildmaster.

" 'Section Forty-seven, Paragraph One,' " Lanzecki intoned without glancing at the panel. " 'In matters of galactic emergency, the Guildmaster may, at his discretion and with due and just cause, conscript the services of any or all active Members for the duration of that emergency.' An emergency situation exists.'' He tapped out another sequence and the Guild bylaw was replaced by a communication dot which enlarged dramatically to reveal its message. Blue Ballybran crystals in octagonal and dodecahedral shapes were in urgent, critical demand as replacements for the great interstellar laser communication devices and certain large drives units.

"They can't all have soured at once," Killashandra said in a voice more grating in snarl than tone.

"The slightest flaw in the crystal focusing coherent light can produce a distortion in communication units. A drive unit or a machine triad could operate without noticeable lapse of efficiency for some time. Not so with the blues. The crystals in the Garthane unit, for example, have been in service for two hundred and five standard years, carrying a total of. . . ."

"Abort your statistics, Lanzecki. Why me? Why must I forego a leave which you know narding well I need. . . ."

Lanzecki inclined his head in recognition of her crystal-soaked fatigue. "I've recalled Formeut, but he is in the Sirius section and even by direct GCS flight cannot be back in less than twenty days."

GCS flight! This *was* an emergency, thought Killashandra, not one bit reconciled to losing her leave time.

"Ballivor is still in the Ranges but his blues are not first quality, nor can he cut in the higher registers. The cuttings you brought in three trips back were flawless and you sing the higher tones. Triads, fifths, octaves are critically needed."

There was nothing in Lanzecki's manner or tone to indicate sympathy with her and yet Killashandra fancied regret flickering in his eyes. She rebelled against the inevitable, as much because she was so desperately weary of crystal that the mere thought of another trip into the Ranges frightened her, as because Lanzecki's arbitrary invocation of a Guild statute exacerbated her natural tendency to be perverse.

"Blue octagons and dodecahedrons, huh? Polyhedrons in

blue!'' She glared savagely at Lanzecki's impassive face. Was the man human or were Guildmasters some sort of construct, programmed with only enough pseudoresponses to counterfeit human behavior? ''Great! And how, pray tell, Guildmaster, do I get them without an operable ship because by all that's holy, nothing in Guild laws can require me to take off in a gyro-soured flitter! That *would* be murder!''

She had the satisfaction of seeing Lanzecki wince. Maybe he was human? She knew, because she'd already checked, that there were no new gyros in Supply: like Ballybran blue polyhedrons, gyros rarely malfunctioned. Ordinarily the gyros could be adjusted and tuned in the course of an ordinary servicing, but some minute structural flaw had now manifested itself in Killashandra's.

''I've got to rest, Lanzecki,'' she said, pleading now. She shoved her hands at him. They were shaking with crystal fatigue. Lanzecki closed his eyes briefly, his mouth stern.

''Get into a radiant bath, Killashandra. I'll send the medic. . . .''

''I don't need a farding medic, Lanzecki. I need off-world!''

''I realize that, Killashandra, far better than you think.''

''Ha!''

The Guildmaster closed his eyes again, recoiling from her venomous rejoinder. Then she'd had enough of him, of crystal, of the Guild, of everything, and she flung herself at and through the door panel.

''Ha!'' The hallway echoed back her explosively bitter syllable. She staggered with exhaustion, careering off the threshold of the grav-lift. It was such a relief to be weightless that she almost went past her dormitory level. Habit, probably, impelled her forward. And down the corridor in the right direction—her feet had been programmed for the route by how many years?—and stopped at the proper door panel. Her name was blazoned there and her right hand lifted, automatically, to the thumb lock. Again, with no direction from her crystal-sound soaked mind, she entered, and dialed for a radiant bath.

She was too weary to strip, not that it made a difference.

She rolled into the tub, the viscous liquid slopping over her as the tank filled rapidly.

"Farding Guild! Them and their polyhedron blues!" She railed at a management that would let itself get into such a short supply state. Not only polyhedron blues but gyros. The Guild could narding well afford to keep a few spare gyros in Supply. . . . And yet, if they had. . . . She wiggled deeper into the warm thick liquid, impatient for the therapeutic soothing.

"I can't go out into the Range again!" she cried in anguish and flailed her hands at the liquid. "I can't. I've got to get off-world. I've got to get relief!"

The bath now enveloped her to her chin and the tingle of crystal sound began to drain from her abused body, lingering on the edge of her bones, on the tips of her nerves, but definitely easing. And with it some portion of her desperation.

Her arms and legs floated idly to the surface, slender but firmly muscled. Objectively she regarded her hands . . . blue dodecahedrons/orthorhombic blues. Cabalistic phrases. She'd have to write them down. In several places or she'd forget.

She brought her arms down in a rejecting *smack* against the radiant liquid; the smart adding fuel to her building fury. She was *not* going out again! Not until she'd been off-world for at least a twenty-day. She couldn't face the isolation of the Milekeys again. Not again! Not so soon!

Ah, but she wouldn't have to, would she? Not until her flitter had been repaired. Bless those gyros! Bless Supply for not having any. Not even the Guildmaster or the GCS Council President could force her into an inefficient craft. Not when it multiplied the chances of scrambling her brains if she got caught in a mach storm! Then where would they get high-register blues? Ha!

These reflections consoled her. She began to relax, letting the radiant ooze seep into her crystal-tired body. Blue orthorhombics . . . ha! She *didn't* have to remember them now! She wouldn't have to go get them. How unusual to be able to forget something you didn't have to remember!

To remember!

Killashandra snorted. Her hands remembered all she really needed to know. How to cut crystal! She held them up, the viscous liquid sheeted from them and she noticed, bemusedly, that the skin was wrinkling into squares, rectangles and triangles, crepey. What had happened to her hands? She submerged them with a limp splash, oddly annoyed at the discovery. The rest of her skin was smooth.

Hands take a lot of abuse in the Range: It wasn't wrinkles at all. Lots of small crystal scars, that's what. She always got good sharp edges to her cuts, sharp enough to slice anything, particularly flesh.

She was too thin again. Well, you forgot to eat at regular intervals when you worked crystals. Eating wasn't a habit of hands; it was metabolic custom.

She'd have time to eat now, wouldn't she?

The bath was cold. She evacuated it and dialed for a second, this time stripping off the remnants of her range suit. Why weren't the radiants eliminating that nardy tingle along her bones, the marrow-deep ache? Once she got rid of that ache. . . . She wouldn't, not until she got off-world. She had to have a chance to think! Without crystal impinging. How could anyone think with that low-constant, bone-conducted ripple distracting you all the time?

Before the third immersion had quite cooled, the medic arrived, and despite her curses, pumped her full of restoratives.

"I don't want energy; I want sleep. I want to get off this farding fool planet and away from you mutes!"

It did her good to scream, but the therapy would have been more beneficial if the deaf medic had been able to react to her vilification. Frustrated, she grabbed his arm, shaking him so that he looked up at her inquiringly.

"I don't want restoratives. I want to sleep. Sleep!"

He nodded, inserted another vial in the barrel of the airgun, shot it, and before she could suitably catalog his antecedents, she'd slipped into deep slumber.

She woke abruptly, knowing by the manner of waking that

she'd been sedated into sleep. She looked at the bed chromo and twenty-six hours had elapsed since she'd been laid there. She wondered what had gone wrong . . . but only briefly, because too many memories flooded back. She cursed viciously because the medic had obviously activated her recall playback. She railed against the Guild for that, too. There were some things, by all that's holy, you don't have to remember! You don't need to remember! You don't want to remember!

Food popped out of the catering slot, giving rise to another flood of Killashandran vituperation. But the choice dishes were her favorites, printed long ago into her private program and guaranteed to stimulate her appetite. She *was* ravenous. With each mouthful she macerated, she chewed out curses for Lanzecki, the Guild, everything.

The playback of recent events, some of which she couldn't imagine why she'd kept, revived perfect recollection of her present dilemma. Twenty-six hours of retrieved data forced back into her crystal-soaked mind. There'd been a time, presumably, when twenty-six hours would've replaced every lost memory. Now it only served to remind her how long she'd sung crystal. Well, the next trip into the Milekeys would erase most of it. Ha! She couldn't take another long trip into the Milekeys, could she, even under Lanzecki's emergency directive, not until her flitter was refitted with operating gyros.

Sated and somewhat mollified by a clear recollection of her recent past, she rose to dress. And stared at the wealth of garments in the closets. The first group were all too familiar, bought at Taliesin and Rommell, and on that dull trip to Buckwell's Star. She pushed them along the slide to the back, out of sight. Now the gaudy gauze of a brilliant purple and fuchsia surtout. . . . The feel of the soft springy fiber in her hand touched a respondent chord, but the memory was elusive. Something pleasurable. To the good. Well then, why hadn't she programmed that into her review?

And this blue-striped affair must reach her ankles, the sleeves hiding her fingers. On what earth had she acquired such a monstrosity? Not her usual choice, certainly, for there'd be no freedom of movement in that constricting thing. It must have been molded to her body. How had she walked? *Had* she walked in it? And where? The faint whiff of perfume stirred an exciting memory. Now why had she edited that from the tape?

Disused memories, exanimate clothing and defunct odors!

She took the gauze from the press and threw its folds around her body. The set was good, she tossed her thick black locks away from her face, and her hair whispered sensuously against the fabric. She found some footwear in purple, obviously bought to match the gown. One cabinet held perfumes in curious flagons and containers, some marked in unfamiliar alphabets with galactic lingua translations in small printing beneath. None of the fragrances matched that clinging to the blue-striped affair. But fragrance dries up. . . . like memories! She shrugged, daubed herself with a spicy mixture that seemed to go with the purple surtout. Her toilet complete, she adjourned to the Guild general hall.

The large, low-ceilinged chamber could have accommodated double the number of active crystal singers and none of the half dozen scattered about the hall looked familiar to her. Not that that actually bothered. The roster of Guild members was subject to change without notice. At one time or another she'd probably met everyone and they, her.

She took a seat in a quiet alcove and dialed the fourth beverage down the caterer, designated a strong euphoric. She recognized the taste as the liquid rapidly dispensed a pleasant lethargy within her. Now, slightly anesthetized to the crystal-echo in other singers' bones, she could contemplate contact.

She wondered who else of the gradually increasing population in the hall were being summarily forced back into the Ranges to work blues. Should she attempt a revolution and the hell with the fecking blue crystals? She was, unfortunately, aware that crystal singers had never struck. The initial part of the recent playback had been a review of Guild Law and history—Lanzecki-inspired, no doubt. He had the advantage of her in this. If she refused to go back out, she could be disbarred from all member privileges and exiled from Ballybran . . . which amounted to slow death. If she weren't a crystal singer, she'd've opted for exile. She might anyhow, just to be difficult. She physically and mentally couldn't face another trip into the Ranges without some respite. But she also knew that however much she might crave surcease from crystal song. she couldn't endure more than a few months away from Ballybran. Crystal was in her blood, her bone, and she required it—symbiotically or parasitically, she had to return to crystal.

However, she could delay as long as possible, with the legitimate excuse of faulty gyros. And the price of blue orthorhombic would rise. Of course, if she delayed too long, Lanzecki could exact a penalty that might whittle down her premiums. She checked through the newly reimpressed knowledge of Guild law and realized that here she did have an advantage. Lanzecki couldn't deduct any penalties, despite the emergency, unless he could prove she was fit and able to perform her Guild duties. And furthermore. . . .

"Killashandra!"

She looked up at the glad exclamation and saw a man in an orange tunic, the shade of which was almost an assault on the eyes, hurrying across the room towards her. His manner was that of an acquaintance of long—and, when he had saluted her with an embrace and kiss, evidently intimate—standing.

"Who the hell are you?"

"Fergil! Don't you remember *me*?" he replied in a tone that suggested she couldn't possibly have forgotten him.

"No, I don't."

Instantly his attractive face evinced surprise, hurt, embarrassment and then tolerant understanding. "Now, Killashandra, you haven't been out in the Range that long this trip. And what brought you back so soon? You swore you'd make enough to go off-world." He'd seated himself as if her invitation were a foregone conclusion. His assurance amused more than it irritated her.

"My gyros are wheezing," she replied in a daunting tone that ought to send him on his way.

He grinned—he had an engaging one, she admitted—and took her hand, stroking her palm in an experienced caress—the sort of caress which she happened to enjoy. She *did* know him? That recall playback had covered nearly ten standard years . . . and there had been no Fergil.

"You really ought to break down and invest in a new flitter," he said briskly, "but you never listen to me."

"Don't I now?"

His fingers ran excitingly up her forearm, where the skin is soft and tender . . . no crystal scars there to deaden sensitivity. Then just as she began to anticipate that stroking, he leaned away from her to dial beverages.

"You're abstemious for someone just in," he remarked. "Try your usual. If your gyros are off, you'll be in for a while."

Well, he knew her favorite form of liquid poison. She raised the goblet in a toast, but she was positive she'd never met this orange man before. Positive. And yet. . . .

"What brings you back in?" she asked, hoping for a lead. "There's no storm warning up."

"You have forgotten. I've been on leave."

"Did Lanzecki call you back?"

"No," he said, in a jocular fashion as if she ought to have known his movements. "As you said, there's nothing on this planet, and I hadn't made enough to go off-world. I just needed," and he gritted his teeth, "to get away from the ranges. . . ." That glowing smile for her again. "And you—" Suddenly he was very serious, a light hand on her arm but a hand which nevertheless warmed into her flesh in a loverly way. "I *know* you are the top crystal singer in the Guild, Killa, but I just don't think we'd last as a duet."

Killashandra stared at him in utter astonishment.

"Duet?"

He waved aside her startled exclamation, turning his head slightly from her in regret. "I've thought a lot about it, Killa. And you're wrong, I'm afraid. Something happens to a man, and a woman, out in the Ranges: something that can set up antagonistic frequencies in your body—as if your very bones hated each other. No," and his smile was tender and full of remorse, "I'd rather we stayed friends . . . loving friends, if you will. You've meant too much to me already to have the memory soured by hatred."

107

Killashandra snorted at his notion of acrimonious memories: of any memories!

"Here, your drink's empty," he said solicitously, taking no notice of her diffident response.

Well, she needed another drink; it went on his tab. And he was rather an incredible personality. How could she have forgotten him? And in presumably a relatively short time. She forced her mind back through the replay to which she'd only a few hours before been subjected. Granted that she had dictated that playback and could have been disenchanted with him at that moment. She could recall descriptions of half a dozen other men but no Fergil with the compelling gray eyes, crisp curling brown hair, and the sure touch of a man who knows how to give pleasure and wants to receive it. More importantly, surely she'd have remembered a man with whom she'd considered doubling. Or maybe that presumption alone had sufficed to censor him. Yes, that was possible. She shook her head, because Fergil had begun to stroke her arm again and she could not ignore the fact that she was positively attracted to him . . . and that she needed relief badly.

He gave it—completely and outrageously—disastrously certain of his ability to arouse and satisfy her. She must have known him!

She would have liked to sleep alone after they made love so that she'd play back the review tape. If she'd censored the Fergil chapter of her life, there'd be a large chronological lapse. . . .

"How long has Fergil been singing crystal, Lanzecki?" Killashandra asked the next day when Fergil had finally quit her side to see to the servicing of his own craft.

"Not too long," Lanzecki replied, in an unusually judicious tone.

"Doesn't he sing well?"

"Yes. Sings well in the higher registers, in fact." Abruptly Lanzecki's face changed and he glanced hopefully at her. "Then you'd consider. . . ."

"Dueting with him?" Killashandra gave a snort of laughter. "Evidently I offered and he . . . refused."

"Really?" Lanzecki stared off into a middle distance. "I must speak to that young man. Supply," he went on in his characteristically neutral manner, "has ordered new gyros for your vehicle on a top priority-emergency basis. They should be here in seven days, plus four to install and tune. . . ."

"Ha! When you need me, Supply hustles, doesn't it?"

"It is not my need, Killashandra Ree. Two GCS drive units have been retuned, but the cuts lowered the range and efficiency by a factor of four. As all the blues used in those drive units were quarries from the Ghange Range at the same time, it is not hard to understand the perturbation which exists over the Guild's inability to furnish immediate replacements."

"I've brought in blues from time to time."

Lanzecki's eyes closed briefly in recognition. "There are very few blue cuttings in the Ranges."

"Nothing more in Ghanges?"

He shook his head. "We've examined that possibility thoroughly."

"I'll just bet you have."

"You must go back to your claim as soon as it is possible." Lanzecki said. "Believe me, I wouldn't risk sending you out if the situation were not so critical."

Though he spoke in his customary neutral tone, something in his manner stopped the sarcastic rejoinder Killashandra was going to make.

"I could almost believe you, Lanzecki," she did say and left.

Out in the hall, she wondered where she could go for eleven days. Nowhere useful. Taliesin was a good four travel days off and she didn't have to check her review tape to know she'd been there often enough to be too well known. Despite Taliesin's proximity, the natives subscribed to the galactic myth that crystal singers seduced people into the Guild. The two main planets of the system were musically inclined civilizations so perfect pitch was not uncommon. And since perfect pitch was a requisite of crystal singing, a good many young people, dissatisfied with Taliesin's limited opportunities, endured the initiation hassle to reap the benefit of high pay and unlimited travel. Taliesin, in her circumstances, was both too far and not far enough.

"Killashandra!" Fergil's delighted greeting was more suitable to an absence of days, not hours. "Where have you been?"

"Getting Lanzecki's bad news."

"What do you mean?" Fergil's pleasure was replaced by concern.

"Eleven days before I'm thrust back into the Range again."

"That's speed!"

"Ha! I can't even get to Taliesin in that time."

"Why would you want to go to Taliesin? If you've eleven days, you can just take off and he can come after you. I know those engineers. . . ."

Killashandra shook her head and answered grimly. "He's invoked Section forty-seven. . . ."

"Section. . . ." Fergil's eyes went blank with the effort to associate. His recall was fresh for he whistled appreciatively in a matter of seconds. "Don't tell me you've got blue cuttings?"

She agreed.

He whistled again, his eyes widening with envy. "Do you know what blues are bringing?"

"There are some things, like scrambled brains, not worth any price."

"Aw, c'mon, Killashandra. A couple crates of those blues. . . ."

"Aw, c'mon, Fergil, you've obviously never cut blues. One of the reasons they bring in such top prices is they're so farding hard to cut. Crack, chip, flaw while you're working. You've got to get deep into the vein before you find any pure stuff. Could take you days and then, up blows a mach storm and shatters the whole face before you can get any real benefit. That is, if you're unfortunate enough to find blues to begin with.''

Fergil waved aside these considerations.. ''Even octagon blues are bringing in a small fortune. I'm going to try prospecting for blues this trip out. There's a bonus posted for any new veins discovered. A good haul of blues and I'm off to Parnell's World.''

Killashandra snorted. She could use a trip to Parnell's World; she'd been there before, because it offered the widest variety of pleasure and vice in the galaxy. It was naturally a favorite destination of crystal singers.

''You could be a rich woman in eleven days, Killa,'' he said with a rueful grin.

''Yeah, rich with addled brains. I'm so farding tired of singing crystal. . . .'' her vehemence startled Fergil. ''I'm as close to crystalizing bone and blood as makes no never mind.'' She rubbed at her arms, unnervingly reassured by the warm flesh she touched.

''Oh, Killa! *You're* far from crystallized,'' Fergil said, an intense gleam in his eyes as he embraced her sensuously.

She pushed away from him, both aroused and annoyed.

''There, there, lover,'' Fergil said, soothingly. He kept hold of one hand. ''Okay, so you've had too much. Just go off-world. How can he stop you?''

''He can and has, and I'd be twice the fool to risk suspension or expulsion.''

Fergil let out a surprised laugh. ''Heptite Guild doesn't expel. . . .''

''They don't have to. They know we can't last without crystal. I remember what happens.'' She gritted her teeth against the memories that flooded, all too unwelcome, into her mind—the ache and throb of crystal-hungry flesh and blood, the excruciating spinal agony that rippled and wrenched you apart. . . . Equally unendurable was the thought of returning to the Ranges, of being submerged so soon again in crystal noise. ''I can't go back, Fergil. I *can't* go back,'' she cried in a voice that was close to a scream.

He gathered her into his arms gently, holding her head into

his shoulder to muffle her hysterical sobs.

"It's too much." Killashandra wasn't certain if she was vocalizing the terror or not. She couldn't go back into the Ranges, not until she'd had some rest, some time away from them. She was sobbing uncontrollably now as Fergil carried her. That was good of him because she didn't have to expend any effort. She hadn't any strength left. Maybe if she collapsed completely. . . .

She was being inserted into a warm radiant bath, the soothing liquid relaxing the taut hysteria of her body.

"You can't send her out in this kind of state, Lanzecki," Fergil was saying at the top of his voice. "She'd crack. She couldn't sing!"

"I've no choice but to send her, Fergil."

"She's got to have some rest."

"Rest she can have. Eleven days of it, but then she has to go out."

"In this condition? Eleven days won't give her enough of a respite, not this close to crystal. You know that."

"I know it, but the situation does not permit exceptions. We must have blues. Of course," and despite her desperate condition, Killashandra caught the change in Lanzecki's voice, "if she will detail the location of her workings. . . ."

With a scream of protest, Killashandra tried to rise from the tub to get at Lanzecki.

"By all that's holy," Fergil was bellowing, "give over her claim? Why, I'd sooner double with her to protect it. . . ."

"By all means do so."

Killashandra had enough strength left to fight off Fergil's hands but she slipped back into the radiant, shrieking curses.

"You won't have to go out alone, Killa. I won't let you go out alone. *I'm* going with you!"

"You're going with me?" Killashandra desisted in her feeble efforts to loosen his hands.

Gently he pulled her into a more comfortable position in the tub, stroking her hair back from her face, deftly wiping some of the liquid from her cheeks and mouth.

"Yes, dear girl, I'm going with you. And we'll cut every barging blue the GCS could use for a thousand years. And

112

then we'll do Parnell's World like it's never been done before! Won't we?''

Compelled by the exultation in those gray eyes, too weary to resist the strength in the comforting hands, Killashandra nodded assent. Before she could gainsay it, a medic had pushed his way to the tub edge and pumped her full of sedatives.

She was kept tranquilized for four days, aired full of high-potency vitamin compounds and anabolics to overcome her pernicious exhaustion. Fergil apparently never left her side for whenever she roused briefly from the euphoric haze, he was there, murmuring soft reassurances, patting her, until the touch of his deft hands became a corollary to her drugged equanimity.

How could she have censored someone like Fergil from her life? Possibly because he was so compatible. And he hadn't wanted to give up his independence, had he? That would have infuriated her. So that would have been why she hadn't wanted to remember the man: her own bruised ego.

She was still bemused when they took off in Fergil's flitter five days later. There'd been an argument between Fergil and Lanzecki: Fergil insisting that she had the right to the eleven full days, with Lanzecki replying that three more of the great interstellar drives had gone sour and that the Guild was under heavy pressure from GCS to get blue dodecahedrons or suffer tremendous penalties. Every singer able to walk was out in the Ranges, trying to find more blues.

"All right, we'll cut your damned dodecs, and then don't try to call us back," Fergil had roared.

"Don't let Killa turn off the storm warnings, Fergil!" was Lanzecki's parting advice.

The first touch of crystal sound as they entered the Ranges brought Killashandra completely out of the thrall of sedation. Her mind was suddenly too clear, like the Milekey's humpy outline against the green sky.

"I'd better fly now, Fergil," she said.

"Now, look, Killa, you're barely. . . ."

"Now, look Fergil, if you think you're going to track back

113

to my blue cuttings when I've scrambled up, think again,'' she said, laughing at the shock in his eyes. ''I've sung crystal too long, young man, not to appreciate your strategy. Well, we'll duet. This time, because I've no guts for the Ranges by myself. But I'll do the piloting.''

Judging by the way he recoiled from her accusation, by the hurt in his darkened gray eyes, maybe she'd done him an injustice. Fergil didn't protest, but he shook his head from side to side as he backed into the furthest corner of the flitter, out of line of sight with any of the directional dials. As a further mute refutation of her indictment, he studied the meteorological charts intently.

Fergil's craft was new, but somewhat sluggish in maneuvering and she tended to compensate, out of habit, for the idiocryncrasies of her ancient flitter. Neither was Fergil accustomed to flying in the Milekeys, to judge by his taut expression as she angled through passes, all but scraping the belly of the vessel on the rocky sides. She dipped low in some canyons, flying their length where speed kept individual markings from being obvious to Fergil. She was feeling much better than she'd expected. True, she was aware of crystal hum along her bones, in her blood, but it wasn't by any means acute.

''Did they pump me fill of depressants?'' she asked Fergil.

''Some. Not enough to worry. Lanzecki and the medics were pretty thick, but I watched and most of what they gave you were standard B complexes and anabolics, plus sedatives to keep you asleep.'' He gave her a cocky grin. ''Must've worked. You're more yourself today, my girl. How's the ship handling? She's packed with stores.''

Killashandra grunted noncommittally and kept her mind on the flying. Occasionally she caught a glint of other flitters in deep canyons as she flew deeper north into the Range.

''Will we have time to cut today?'' he asked casually after they were two hours in flight.

''Should do.''

They were nearly to the place, she realized, feeling the answering resonance in her body. She wondered how she could tune her body so selectively: one time to the yellows, another to the rose quartz, and now to the elusive blues. Once a singer had worked a cutting several times, he could always find his way back.

So she flew up and west, to confuse Fergil. There was a long low canyon, one of the major fissures of the range, leading up to her cutting. She'd fly over it, swing round and come back at the furthest end, where the black crag cut off the rest of the trough. Of course, let him mark the black cliff, a seemingly distinctive landmark. Milekey had hundreds such. He'd learn soon enough.

She glided in, right over the crag, observing him glance up. Then he also saw where she intended to touch the flitter down and he blanched noticeably.

"Easy as she goes," Killashandra said, having neatly aligned the craft with the marks left by her own flitter.

"I didn't think you'd manage that," Fergil said, his eyes dancing with admiration though his voice was full of relief.

Killashandra laughed, pleased with her expertise. "A few surprises in the old gal yet, aren't there?" But suddenly, her doubts and fancies about him dissipated and she felt comfortable again with him. She unlatched her sonic cutter, motioned for him to do the same. "Grab a container," she added, as she undogged the hatch and stepped, carefully, onto the narrow ledge. The inadequate landing space was one of the reasons she'd not worked this cutting more often.

Fergil gave the nauseating drop a passing glance and followed, hefting crate and cutter easily.

Sun glinted off the blue crystal rock laid bare of its encrustment of machstorm-driven debris and abrasions. Fergil whistled appreciatively, leaned closer and ran a speculative hand down the obvious axial flaws.

"Polyhedron blues! A mountain of them."

"Let's see can we carve a few triads out of this face," Killashandra suggested and sang out an A. She gestured for him to sing a third above or below. He'd a good strong voice—not a vibe off pitch—and then the chord answered them from the mountain. Both had their cutters tuned when Killashandra's hand found the resonating section of crystal. She was still singing her note as she made the first cut but he hadn't her breath support. He'd learn.

They cut quickly; he was good and his sonic cutter was not a fraction of an inch behind hers as they sliced blue crystal from parent rock. She finished the outer edge cuts and turned off her cutter before she realized that his was still on. . . . He stood, transfigured by the feel of vibrating crystal in his hand. She knew the sensation. Knew too well the insidious, mind-sapping joy of it. How long had Fergil been singing crystal? She snatched the orthorhombic from his hand and watched him snap out of the trance, snarling with anger.

"You can do that as long as you want on your own time, Fergil. We're here to cut crystal, not be seduced by it. Finish off the shape."

He shook his head. "Sorry, Killa. I forgot."

She felt his crystal pulsing in her hand, in harmony with the one she'd just cut. She handed it back to him before she was entranced. "Shape it. Now! I'm watching." He all but wrenched the polyhedron from her. "You haven't been out that often, have you?"

"That much, too much! What does it matter? I sing well, don't I?" He spun on her angrily, the cutter raised almost threateningly. He completed the cuts in a savage way and then placed the dodecahedron carefully in the crate. "Where now?" There was no expression at all in his face and suddenly Killashandra was afraid that she'd alienated him. She was desperate for the reassurance of his smile. Then he relaxed and grinned sheepishly.

She took a deep breath and sang out a C sharp. He belted out a respectable F sharp and they touched the resonating area at the same instant. They were cutting well when suddenly the sound distorted on her blade as the blue shattered down its longest axis. She switched off her cutter just in time to prevent his crystal from cracking with the dissonance. He was as unnerved by the break but kept to his cut, finishing deftly.

"Now what?" he asked her as he laid the F sharp in the protective foam sheath. "That's only happened to me once before."

They both regarded the long fracture with disgust.

"It happens most frequently cutting blues," she said, glaring angrily at the half won C sharp. "We can cut further down the face," and she gestured to the dull, pitted face, "but we've got to cut away a lot of junk first. Or we can suffer the noise and take this out down below the flaw."

Fergil rubbed the side of his face by his ear, as if in anticipation of the aural distress. "How good's this face? Worth wasting the effort if it fractures again?"

Killashandra shrugged. They weren't really far enough past the surface to tell. "You get the largest percentage of defects on the outside, of course. . . ."

"Let's try once more to cut here." Fergil raised his tool.

They did and got a good triad before a vertical flaw developed.

"I've a hunch we should keep on at this face though," Killashandra said, strewing the shattered fragments of the imperfect crystal down the precipice.

"I've not sung crystal long enough to argue," Fergil said, grinning cheerfully at her as he wiped the sweat from his forehead.

His candour reassured her as much as his subtle compliment.

"We'll play my hunch, at least for today, then."

They ran across one other short fissure which ruined a tonic octave. Once past that, she could tell from the ring, mountain deep, that they were on to a fine, pure vein.

"Enough to buy Parnell's World at current prices," she told Fergil and laughed at the anticipatory gleam in his eyes. "The trouble is we wouldn't live long enough to cut it all."

"Why not?" Fergil demanded with a bark of exultant laughter. "Singers can last forever if they're good. . . ."

"If they're lucky. . . ."

He swung on her. "You're good, one of the best, and you've been singing for. . . ."

"Enough!" Suddenly she didn't want to *know*, and it angered her to think that he knew. "I'm still singing. And let's stop chattering and start cutting. That's what we're here for."

She belted out a G and they cut a five note dominant before

crystal began to murmur evening song.

That night, Killashandra would have preferred solitude to ponder some of the contradictions in Fergil but, as if he sensed her disquiet, he distracted her with loverly nonsense and skillful lovemaking. It was one thing to listen to night crystal song by yourself: quite another to hear the same serenade over the roar of the blood at climax. And very flattering to hear a man's voice crying out his pleasure in you. Killashandra'd forgotten that facet of singing duet.

By high noon the next day, they had to work with blinder-slits, but the cuttings were fabulous. No partner could have been as good as Fergil now he'd hit his stride. Whatever her reservations had been the previous day, his performance now dispelled them. His voice and hers blended, caught resonances that could be heard echoing four canyons beyond: his cutter worked as swiftly and surely as hers, instinctively finding the axes of the octagons and dodecahedrons, producing symmetrical sets as neatly as she did. She was quite ready to concede that they two might well level the blue mountain when the alarms began.

"Hey, that's the dew bell!"

"In weather like this!" Killashandra swung round to the northwest. No storm sign there at all. "Keep cutting. It's only a dew bell."

He finished the cut he was on, but when she started to sing another he yanked her cutter from her.

"Lanzecki warned me specifically about you and storm signals."

"Look, I've sung crystal long enough to know safety margins. Something in here tells me when to go. That's why I've kept my wits." She glanced at the half-full container. "The dew bell only means alert. And we can finish that out."

He shook his head and motioned her to the flitter.

"You nardy fool! Give me back my cutter!" She made a grab for it. He stepped into the flitter with the cutters just as another warning sounded.

"Several hours, huh?" he taunted, keeping his body between her and the narrow path to the flitter's portal as he heaved the half-full crate into the lock. "We've four crates and no more time, Killashandra. That mountain's not going anywhere.''

"The storm'll change the frequencies, flaw the surface," she shrieked. "We've cut deep. It could fissure and crack the mother rock." She flung a protective arm against the face they'd been working so successfully. "We've thirds and fifths. Two full octaves. Please, Fergil? Just one more. I've got to get off this barfing world! I've got to!''

He hesitated for a fraction, twisting his head at the siren gleam of resonating blue crystal. If she could just edge past him to the flitter. . . .

He caught her shoulder full with a narcotic blast, and she hadn't time to curse him before unconsciousness overwhelmed her.

"I had to do it, Killa," someone was saying. "Lanzecki told me how you'd act. Killa! Killa?''

She tried to strike out at him as consciousness returned but she was strangely hampered. And woke completely to find herself up to the neck in a hot radiant bath, Fergil crouched by the tub edge, holding her head out of the liquid.

"You misbegotten, sterile offshoot of degenerate perverts with blurred chromosomes from an outcasts' planet . . . if you don't leave me alone, I'll warp you into early senility.''

"Killa! I had to. The storm was a variant. We nearly didn't get out of the Milekeys at all. If you'd been in your flitter. . . .''

"Leave the boy alone, Killashandra. He's settled an old account of yours," Lanzecki's face appeared beyond Fergil's shoulder. "There are nine scrambled singers lost in the Milekeys in this storm. If you hadn't been paired with Fergil, you'd've been one, too.''

"And you'd've lost your blues, wouldn't you? That's all you care about really, Lanzecki! Isn't it?''

She was screaming the last words because the crystal pain in her bones began to grab at her spine. She had gone back into the Ranges too soon.

"Where's the barfing medic?" she shrieked, writhing.

"What's the matter with her, Lanzecki?" cried Fergil.

The concern in his voice, the way he swung accusingly at the Guildmaster was balm to Killashandra's soul. But the expression on Lanzecki's face, almost pitying, was the final outrage.

"Get out of here, Lanzecki!" She grabbed at his hand at the same time, so he'd feel the crystal shock coursing through her body, so he'd have a taste experientially of what the farding Guild was demanding of her. "You forced me back too soon. How d'you like a taste of it?" To her surprise, Lanzecki stoically endured her grasp. It was Fergil who broke her hold and then dropped her hand as if it had burned him.

"What's wrong with her?" Fergil demanded.

"Sometimes," Lanzecki said in a soft distant tone, "a singer seems to be keyed into the last crystal he'd cut before a storm, and experiences the storm, too."

"*Where's that medic, Lanzecki?*"

The man appeared suddenly and Killashandra felt the coolness of air pressure and the merciful oblivion.

"You can't ask her to go out again, Lanzecki. You can't!" Fergil's voice was stern. He was a good man, Killashandra thought, standing up against Lanzecki, against his own Guildmaster. She wasn't really concerned, though, with the argument going on over her limp body.

When Lanzecki answered, also from a distance, his voice was dull and lifeless. "She's the only one cutting blues, Fergil."

"We brought in close to four crates. . . ."

Lanzecki gave a mirthless snort. "When we need forty to ease the emergency?"

"Forty?" Fergil's voice strangled on the repetition.

Killashandra let herself slip back into oblivion. Fergil was her champion. She could rest. She had to rest. For some reason that escaped her. . . .

She was conscious first of the ache in her bones and the soreness that tenanted her entire body. She tried to ignore that, thinking beyond herself to externals and felt . . .

warmth of another body. The warmth . . . the comfort . . . the sensation of an arm around her waist, limp-handed, but the fingers loosely laced through hers. Puzzled, she moved slightly to peer at the face, but the room was dark. Carefully, she inched her free arm forward, pressed the bedlight and saw the ugly-attractive face of the man sleeping beside her. Strange.

She must have been out in the Ranges a long time for the ache to be still with her. Usually, three or four radiant baths sufficed to remove the worst of it. Who was this man? It was undeniably comfortable in his arms, and she felt protected. A nice, unusual feeling. Obviously he was no stranger to her, or her bed. They fitted too comfortably together.

She wriggled closer . . . and he roused.

He had gray eyes. That was right, but something in her look must have alerted him.

"Have you forgotten me again, Killashandra? I'm Fergil. And really, my dear girl, if you keep on forgetting me like this I shall be hurt."

"Fergil?" The name did have a familiar taste in her mouth. "Oh, Fergil!" And she burrowed into the safe, remembered arms as all too painful memories surged back at his cues.

He held her, comforting her and she knew now why she ached so and what was in store for her. And Fergil. And she dreaded the Ranges and then suddenly, did not. Fergil would be with her, and memories that were pleasant reviewed themselves. As long as she had Fergil with her she could remember things easily. Memory now was far more preferable to blank ignorance.

The storm had blown itself out finally the morning Lanzecki came by to inquire about her progress.

"I'm the only one singing blues, aren't I?" Killashandra asked the Guildmaster.

He nodded.

"Lanzecki, she's not well enough to sing crystal yet," Fergil said, throwing a protective arm about her shoulders.

"She is the only one singing blues. . . ."

"You said you'd mobilized every singer to prospect. . . ."

"So I have. Anyone who can handle a cutter is out in the Ranges now and Killa. . . ."

"Haven't you recalled Formeut. . . ?" Fergil sounded desperate.

"He's en route, but the situation worsens. . . ."

"Killashandra brought you in three and a third crates. . . ."

"As I told you then, we require forty at the bare minimum. . . ."

"She can't possibly cut forty crates. . . ."

The Guildmaster drew himself up. "Unless Killashandra operates her own claim, I am empowered to obtain its direction so that. . . ."

"No one works my claim but me!" Killashandra struggled to her feet, shaking now with anger rather than crystal shock.

Fergil thrust his body between her and Lanzecki. "How the flaming hell can you rationalize that in Guild Law?" Fergil was furious, too. "It's her right. . . ."

"Which can be set aside with due cause. . . ." Lanzecki held out a plastic flimsy on which were impregnated the GCS seals.

With a sinking terror, Killashandra knew she had no alternative now.

"He's bluffing," Fergil cried. "He's trying to murder you."

"He's not bluffing," Killashandra said, dully staring at the flimsy, but she didn't refute the second charge.

"I'm not trying to murder her either, Fergil," Lanzecki said in a weary tone, "because I am within my authority to insist that you double with her again. The sooner you two can cut the required quota the sooner this," and he shook the flimsy, "can be destroyed and . . . forgotten."

"Easily forgotten!" said Killashandra in a barking sneer. "But you overlook one factor, Lanzecki. What if the storm has split the mountain to shards?" and she devoutly wished it true.

The Guildmaster shuddered, his eyes closing as if fearful

that the mere mention of such a possibility could bring it about.

"From what Fergil said, the mountain is pure crystal. It won't have been affected by the storm as much as a thinner vein might."

"What if it is, Lanzecki?" Killashandra could not resist taunting him. "What does GCS do then?"

"*Then*,"—and Lanzecki called her bluff,— "every singer concentrates on your claim until they recover the pure vein if they have to dig to plasma." His manner was implacable. "Spare me further puerile divagations. Killashandra has the only blue workings: She is to cut there as long as she is able. Otherwise other singers will be sent to the claim."

"And how could you bloody well find that claim, I want to know?"

"There *are* ways," Lanzecki told Fergil, "tedious but ultimately successful. And you are to guard her life with yours, Fergil. You will obey, instantly, any storm warning and leave from the Range. But . . ." and there was no doubting Lanzecki's meaning, "do not leave the Range without due cause or you both suffer expulsion."

"Death either way, Lanzecki!" cried Fergil, but Lanzecki had gone. Fergil grabbed Killashandra into the protective circle of his body. "You can't go!"

She pushed him away and reached for a Range suit. "He means it, Fergil. I've no choice but by all that's holy on every planet in this galaxy, I'm the only one who will cut my claim as long as I can keep my wits!" A deep abiding fury strengthened Killashandra now and Fergil noted the change in her with reluctant approval.

"And I'll make sure you keep your wits for years to come," he cried, responding to the challenge. Then, as if he could not bear their separation any longer, he grabbed her back into his arms. "You're the most fantastic woman. . . ." His voice was shaking with pride, admiration . . . and love.

Although Killashandra's flitter had been repaired, they took off again in his. The false energy of wrath deserted her once they were airborne, and at the moment Fergil turned expectantly to her.

"You'd better take the controls now, Killa."

"Why? You flew her back!" That small snake of doubt nipped at the heels of her trust in Fergil. All the long moment he stared at her incredulously, she realized that he hadn't been at her claim long enough, nor had he sung crystal long enough, to be drawn back by a familiar resonance.

"There was a storm blowing up, Killa," he said, gently, ruefully. "I turned on the homer and pushed the ship as fast as she'd move. In fact,"—and he shrugged regretfully, "I had to dump all our stores to lighten her for additional speed. I sure as hell had no spare time to mark the way."

Since she'd seen Supply loading stores and yet they'd been full four days before on their first trip out, she had to concede that point and slowly took the pilot chair. Ingrained caution dictated another route into the Range, coming down a different trough, up over the ridge separating it from the major fissure and the black crag. Only there wasn't much left of it. She didn't mention its loss nor, apparently, was Fergil aware of the alteration in the landscape.

And there had been several. For one moment, as she got an unobstructed view of her mountain, Killashandra experienced a moment of pure terror—that the blue crystal lode had been storm-blasted: That her wish had become fact. But the answering note in her bones was clear and unsullied despite the fact that half the adjoining promontory had fallen atop the narrow ledge by the cutting and generously enlarged it. The face they'd been working was blackened and pitted by the storm's violence: no one in passing would have known what lay behind that scarred rock.

"How do you *know* this is the right place?" Fergil asked, completely disoriented.

"You feel it," she replied with the abrupt rudeness of experience in the face of ignorance.

"Feel it?"

"In your bones!" She laid her hand on his and this time he didn't jerk it away. He blinked, frowned, and then recognition widened his eyes with astonishment.

"Is that how you know?"

"You haven't cut crystal long enough."

"No, Killashandra, I haven't. You," and he caressed her cheek gently, his eyes soft, "shepherded me my first time into the Ranges. Oh, I know you've forgotten," he said with a half-apologetic grin, "probably because I was such a right dolt."

"Well, you learned in a helluva hurry then, because you cut damned good duet with me," she replied. "Speaking of which, let's cut Lanzecki's fecking blues."

"Right! The more we do the sooner we can get off this crazy-cracked ball of sound, to Parnell's World together and then . . ." his voice dropped to a vibrant suggestive note that made her laugh.

"Then let's sing crystal and cut the agony short!"

And how they sang the blues. The pure mountain had held. Once they cut away the storm-blasted layer, the crystal sang true, resounding across the storm-widened canyon, until the ache of the faultless sound reached the limits of the bearable. But Killashandra endured because she had to, and because somehow Fergil made it supportable.

They cut three crates the first day: working until the ping of crystal cooling in the twilight made tuning impossible. And then they lay in each other's arms, too weary for loving, too keyed to the mountain to sleep until it, too, had hushed.

As long as she was actively cutting, the crystal pain was neutralized. Nonetheless by the third day, Killashandra asked Fergil what he'd brought in the way of depressants. With pity in his eyes, he gave her a dose. The fifth day she injured herself badly, slicing away the fleshy part of her thumb. Fergil mouthed requisite reassurances, but she could see that he was annoyed because they'd lost both of the huge dodecahedrons they'd been cutting.

She insisted that he permaflesh her hand, and dose her with pain-relievers so she could continue working. Perversely she was irritated because he tacitly accepted her sacrifice.

The sixth day he wouldn't give her any more depressants because he said that was why she'd cut herself: Her reactions were too slow. She screamed that she couldn't stand the pain until he did give her a half dose. She didn't cut as well and bollixed four small cuttings. That night she tried to find out where he hid the drugs and moaned through a sleepless night without surcease while he snored with exhaustion.

The seventh day dawned with a stifling heat, the sort that precedes a break in weather. She began to cut with a frantic intensity, seemingly able to avoid all kinds of minor disasters through speed alone. But the pace told on Fergil and she blasted him for the novice he was; taunting him that a really experienced singer could keep up with her, crippled and crystal-crazed as she was.

"Crazy, is right," he shouted back at her. "No sane person cuts as fast as you do."

"I've got to cut fast. There's storm coming!"

Immediately alert, Fergil cocked his head for the flitter's alarms. "Did you short 'em off? Did you?" he cried, shaking her when she didn't answer him. When she denied turning the alarms off, he wouldn't believe her and, despite her curses and threats, he dashed into the flitter to check.

"It's the weather. I know! I can feel the storm coming. I don't need alarms, you stupid twit! I've cut crystal long enough!"

"The charts say we've twelve clear days . . ." he bellowed from the flitter, brandishing the meteorology flimsies at her.

"The variant storm, you numskull, changes any pattern," she yelled back. "Those nardy charts aren't worth the plastic they're printed on. Move yourself out here and cut! Damn you! Cut!"

He came and worked grimly beside her until his voice was ragged and harsh when they pitched a cut. But with each crystal they cut, Killashandra reckoned that she was that much closer to peace, to tranquillity in blood and bone, to a long, long journey away from crystal.

The next octagons cut were flecked with bloodstains: Fergil's and hers. She wouldn't even give him time to get permaflesh from the flitter. He cursed once the cutters were tuned, cursed in tempo to the diabolical pace she was setting. They had just carved a match double fifths which finished off a crate when Fergil took her by the arm.

"Nothing's worth this pace, Killa. Slack off! We'll kill ourselves."

She wrenched free, her sweeping glance of him deriding his weakness. "I've only today. The storm'll be here soon."

Before she could inhale to sing the cutting note, the dewbell clanged.

"Impossible!" Fergil said it like a prayer, dashing to the skimmer.

"Come back here and cut, you fool. It's only the dewbell. We've time."

"You said the variant storm changed everything," Fergil replied, heaving the first crate into the lock. "I just got us out of here last time because I made you come at the dew bell."

"Come back here and cut!"

"Forget the nardy cutting! Help me load."

"There aren't enough yet," she cried, counting the crates as she passed them to him. How many had they already stored in the cargo bay? She couldn't rightly remember. "There aren't enough yet. I've got to cut enough this time." She picked up her cutter again and dashed back to the cliff. She cleared her throat and reached for a high G. Her voice gave before she could tune the cutter. Startled, because her voice had never betrayed her, she swallowed several times, took a good deep breath, pressed against her diaphragm and sang out. Again her voice wavered and cracked. "Fergil. Sing it for me!"

The high clear D was almost drowned out by additional klaxons from the skimmer. But she caught the pitch and tuned her cutter.

"C'mon, Fergil," she yelled over the piercing cry of crystal. "We've time for one more!"

"That's the girl, Killa," Fergil called back merrily. "Cut the next one for me. Your voice'll recover. Just keep cutting. Lanzecki said to leave at the dewbell. Remember? I'll be back. Yes, indeed. I'll be back."

His farewell suddenly penetrated the fogs of her fatigued mind. She turned and stared at the flitter.

"Wait for me, will you, Killashandra?" he cried, waving. His mocking laugh and his words made sudden, horrible sense.

She threw aside the cutter with a snarl and raced down the track they'd worn, but the skimmer's hatch closed before she could reach it. The suction of takeoff pushed her back, almost to the edge of the precipice. She fell to her knees in the rubble, unable to believe that Fergil was abandoning her! And abruptly as certain that that had been in his mind all along. Weeping, she acknowledged both betrayal and abandonment. With an awful clarity she knew what she had tried to rationalize, that she never had met Fergil until the day he had insinuated himself into her presence in the hall. He'd banked, and accurately, on the fact that someone who'd sung crystal as long as she would have erratic recall, even with the help of a playback. He must've known of the emergency before he approached her, counting on Lanzecki's unwilling cooperation. Had Lanzecki betrayed her, too, for the Guild's need?

She didn't feel the wind rising, the enormity of the double treachery dulling her sensation of physical buffets. It was the moan of crystal all around that roused her. The moan and the cessation of pain within her.

Utterly calm, she rose to her feet, incuriously noticed the roiling blackness of the swiftly descending storm. Why had she never appreciated the beauty of a mach storm? She became fascinated by its incredible speed, the look of unlimited power in the billowing mutiplicity of black, ochre, and gray clouds. The moan intensified into a low shriek, then broke into chords, dissonances, harmonies as the storm winds caressed music from the living rock.

Her body arched with the sonic ecstacy which engulfed her. She began to sing, as her ear remembered melodies composed by the infinite chords around her. Arias seemed to crash into the canyons and symphonies leaped across peaks, bombarding her with ever more diabolically increased tempi, with rhythms that made her sway and whirl in time. She sang, and the whole blue crystal mountain answered her in a magnificently throated chorale.

The blue mountain! That was all Lanzecki had wanted of her. And Fergil. And Lanzecki had sent Fergil with her: certain that the traitor would get enough of the blue resonances on this second trip to bring him unerringly back to the parent sound. And for good measure, Fergil would have her dead body to mark the spot. For she'd never last the storm alive.

So she was to mark the spot? Not if she could prevent it.

The mountain was singing such a fortissimo that she didn't need to pitch the cutter: She'd only to turn it on.

At the top of her lungs, playing her voice up and down an incredible span, she attacked the crystal face with the cutter, slicing irrespective of axes: hearing the satisfactory scream of the abused crystal as she hacked a way into the mountain.

"Abuse me, would he?" she chanted. "Use me, would he?"

She'd alter the frequencies for him so he'd never find his way back to her pure-hearted mountain. The storm-stroked crystal obligingly fell away in great rectangles from her ruthless assault. With an hysterical strength, she pushed aside, knocked over, crawled past crystal spires and spikes, and made herself a tomb deep in the heart of sound.

The mach storm seduced ever louder, weirder symphonies from the willing rock as it rolled over her blue sepulcher. And Killashandra, bone and blood vibrating to the phenomenon, willing, delivered her soul to the sound of death.

Gene Wolfe

THAG

ONCE upon a time there was a boy named Eric who had a tame raven and a ragged cap and no boots, and lived with his mother in a cottage in the forest. Eric and his mother were very poor, but nonetheless they possessed a great treasure, a charm ancient and powerful. This was a bear's skull, and it hung from the roofbeam of their little house on a chain of iron. Eric's great-grandfather had made it long ago, choking the bear with moonlight and filling his skull with the cottony tales of rabbits, and the urine of shadows, and black feathers snatched at great risk from the left foreleg of an eagle, and many other things. The bear's skull was the home of Thag, as a beehive is the home of bees; and Thag was a powerful spirit though he was often away.

One day when Eric and his mother were picking mushrooms in the damp spring woods, he asked her to tell him—again—about the last time Thag had returned home; for this had been the winter after Eric was born, and he had been too small to remember. So Eric's mother told him, and it was a story that grew better with each telling, just as the hilt of a scramasax learns to glow beneath its owner's hand. For Eric's father had, with the aid of Thag, made the trees to dance down the highroad, and built a great hall of glass on Nine Men's Meadow through whose dome the stars could be seen by daylight, and forced certain rich men in the town to disgorge a part of what they had won by law from the poor country folk, and for this last, after Thag had gone again, had been hanged.

There had been a great fair on the gallows hill (as Eric's mother explained to him) for the hanging, with jugglers and gingerbread, and beer given free so that men filled their caps with it and set them on their heads. She and Eric had been the cynosure of all eyes, the only time in her life that she had felt so important, so that she swore if she could she would marry tomorrow if only her new husband could be hanged too; and it was then that Eric decided that if ever Thag came home to the bear's skull again he would use him, and surpass all the exploits of his father, both for wonder and boldness.

Now that very night Thag returned. Eric was lying asleep in his little three-sided loft beneath the roof when he dreamed he saw a running man in crimson and gold who carried a naked falchion. Eric knew it was the custom of Thag to appear as a man in dreams and otherwise in reality, and he knew that this was Thag. Behind Thag, very dimly seen and small in the distance, were three figures; but Eric paid them little attention. He woke, and the whole house was quiet as the wind in the wood. Then Gnip, the raven, stirred on his perch and said, "Mystery," and Eric heard a humming in the bear's skull outside his window and knew Thag was back. In the morning it would be necessary to propitiate Thag, and then he could do whatever he wanted.

Now the king of that country was named Charles the Wise, and he was sleeping late of the morning following the day following the night Thag had returned at last, when he was waked all at once by three things together. The first was that the queen ran into his bedroom screaming; and the second was a great shouting in the bailey, accompanied by the clashing and smashing heard when polearms and partisans and halberds and brown bills are let fall to the cobbles; and the third was that the whole castle had begun to rock back and forth beneath him, so that when he looked out the window he saw the watchtower tossing against the sky like the mainmast of a galleass in a gale. Then the queen (a tall, fair, fine-featured woman just settling into solid flesh after her girlhood, with no more brains than a sack of groats) cried, "Charles, save me!" and when he asked her what was wrong she explained that they were set upon by the mitred powers of Hell, and every knight in the castle who could throw a leg over a horse was already ten days' ride off, and the men-at-arms had dropped them and were hiding in the cistern, and the archers were all unstrung as well. And she concluded by saying that if he did not flee this minute they were doomed.

Then the king took thought, and particularly upon his father's maxim, given him when he was but young, that kings sat three-legged stools—the legs being their armies, their castles, and their treasuries. And it came to him that as his army was already scattered, if he should leave his castle and the gold and silver therein he should have nothing and would be a king no longer. And also that the tax rolls of the kingdom were long and complex, and the windings of the castle passages of great elaboration; and that the conquerors (whoever they were) might welcome someone who could explain these things, and that in time they might even be persuaded to go a-conquering elsewhere leaving the affairs of this kingdom in the hands of that trusty vassal Charles, who was already so well suited to direct them. And so he bade the queen drink a flacon of wine and be quiet, and dressed himself in hose, and a jerkin rich and impressive but without presumption, and went out to confront his conquerors. But he found no one there but Eric.

"Well," said the king, "how do you do, boy? Where has everyone gone?"

"I believe most of them have run away," Eric told him. "But a good many have been eaten." Then the raven, Gnip, came and settled on his shoulder.

The king dropped to his knees at once. "I perceive you are a magician," the king said, "and that that bird is your puissant familiar; and I confess that it has always seemed to me that were I a magician I would choose to return to that very age at which you manifest yourself; but I would think you must find the raiment you have selected rather chill—I can show you better."

In this way Eric became ruler of the country, and after giving his mother a kingdom of her own (and then shutting her up in a bottle because she would not stay there) reigned without aging at all for thirty years, at the end of which time the realm was a wilderness. Deer ran through the streets of the town, and few there were to loose an arrow; wolves bred in wineries, and foxes in farrowing pens; undines from the sea came up the river ten leagues beyond the ford; the stonetrolls of the mountains were seen on the roads at noon; and goblins, excessively ugly and evil, with seventeen fingers on each hand and steel teeth, stood guard at the castle barbican. Throughout all this Eric was, needless to say, exceedingly happy.

As for Thag, he had taken the dungeons for his own, but came out promptly whenever he was wanted and occasionally when he was not. He took the forms of a black and reeking mist, a crab covered with living slime, a dog with its fur afire, a fountain of sand, and many other things; and when Eric rode out hunting—on a unicorn or a hippogryph as often as not—he sometimes noticed that the castle was coming to resemble the skull of a bear, but it did not disturb him at all.

King Charles (who had often assured Eric that his name was *the foolish*) stayed on with his queen, they having become Eric's principal servitors (Thag excepted), and rejoiced in the possession of a son called Prince Robert who was the rightful heir, though he scarcely knew it. And while the king often mourned in secret for the palmy days of his pride, he comforted himself with the knowledge that he still commanded his castle and treasure—Eric had hardly spent a cent.

Thus matters stood, until one evening when Eric was dining in the great hall by the light of a single guttering candle on a golden pricket, there appeared from nowhere three remarkable figures. The first was a blonde girl of great beauty, who wore a diaphanous gown that left one breast bare. The second was a darkhaired woman, also of great beauty, with a white forelock that made Eric think of a night sky slashed by lightening; this woman was dressed in a white robe embroidered with gold, and carried a staff forked at the top like the horns of a bull. The third was a man, tall and muscular, gray-bearded and one-eyed. And as this man, the last of the three, appeared, there came from the dungeons a roar of anguish.

Eric saw at once that these were not common folk (or he would have had them devoured), and rose and introduced himself and offered to share his dinner with the newcomers; but he had no sooner done this than his pet (ravens are long-lived birds—sometimes inconveniently so) came flapping in at a window and lit on the one-eyed man's shoulder.

"Now," the one-eyed man said, "I see we are in some kind of castle," and he began to examine the hangings and decorations, as if he were leaving everything to the woman with the staff.

"I heard Thag roar," she said, "at the moment we materialized. How long has he been here?"

"Thirty years," said Eric, so surprised that he never considered not answering.

"Time flies rapidly here, then," the one-eyed man commented. He had taken down a broadspear from the wall, and was fingering the edge as he spoke. "I thought we were close upon Thag."

"We were," the woman told him, "but as you say, time can pass quickly here—thirty years between paragraph and paragraph, if need be."

"What do you mean?" asked the man, but before she could answer him the king and queen entered, followed by Prince Robert. They had been watching from an alcove, and the king (who was of the old belief, as the mighty usually are whether or not they will admit it) had decided to throw his sword.

"Great Woden," he said, "we cast ourselves upon your mercy, and on the mercy of serene Frigg and lovely Freya. The throne of this land is mine, mine to hold in my lifetime, mine to give by father-right to my son when I die. For half again a score of years have I been defrauded of it—slay the monster and grant me justice."

And Woden said, "What the Hell is he talking about?"

and as he spoke the keystone of the great arch of the castle cracked, and a little sliver of stone no bigger than a fingernail fell ringing to the floor.

"He thinks we're the Norse gods," the woman said, and the girl added, "Don't you see, Daddy, we're in a book."

"That's impossible."

"Not more impossible than going backward in time. Look around at things: There's the evil magician—that boy in the pointed hat—here's the castle; there's the true king, the fat lady is the queen, and that fellow who hangs his head and snivels is the prince. Thag is the monster in the crypt beneath the castle. We kill him and disappear, the magician gets pushed off a roof or something, and that's the end."

Eric asked, "Are you saying that we are people in a book in whatever place you come from?"

The one-eyed man nodded. "That's what they're saying— a fairytale—I'm not sure I believe it." He paused. "Are you well-read? At least by whatever standards are used here?"

Eric nodded. "I've spent many happy hours in the castle library—it's something we enchanters are expected to do, and I've come to enjoy it."

"Then tell me something. Do the characters in the books you have here ever read themselves?"

Eric shook his head. "Never, to my knowledge. They're always going somewhere."

"That might be it, then. In our world, you see, it would be quite possible for a character in a book to sit peacefully before his fire reading the short stories of Alexander Solzhenitsyn." Just at that instant Thag rushed into the room in the form of a headless bear, blood spurting from the stump of his neck. "Do I kill him?" Woden asked Frigg.

"A moment ago I would have said yes."

The bear stood upright before the one-eyed man, blood cascading over his shoulders and his extended paws.

"Now you don't—why not?"

Freya-goldenhair touched his arm. "It will be the end of the story, won't it, Daddy? And if we can't be killed, how can Thag? He's been here thirty years now, they say. Won't this just turn him loose to go somewhere else?"

"I don't think this is where he really belongs," the woman called Frigg said. "This is probably a very low energy level for him, as it is for us. And he's asking you to do it, standing there with his chest exposed like that—if he's not begging you not to. I don't like it."

"Then the thing to do is to keep him here." Like a fisherman impaling a pike, Woden drove his spear into the bear's hind foot, pinning it to the oak floor of the hall. "Make it tight," the woman called Frigg advised him, and with a spiky morgenstern he pounded the iron-shod shaft until the head was nearly buried in the wood.

"Use him for your spells all you want," the one-eyed man told Eric, "but if you let him go now I think he'll disappear on you, and I know damned well I'll come back here and make you sorry you did."

Eric bowed. "I understand, Magister."

(Frigg whispered to Freya, "There has to be a world that corresponds to each of our fictions, dear, since what never was nor will be is inconceivable. Still, I wonder what Thag really is." And the bear became a snake pinned by the tail and struck an inch short of her heel.)

"Magister," Eric asked as the one-eyed man began to melt into the air, "what shall I call you? You said you are not Woden?"

"My name is Harry Nailer."

Eric bowed again. "Harry Nailer. It is fitting, Magister." He was already thinking of the things he would do to the king.

And as soon as the three were gone he did them; and lived, in the most literal sense of the words, happily, ever, after.

Edgar Pangborn

MAM SOLA'S HOUSE

THE two-sided image gazed into Patric Jonz from the window of an odd-goods shop, as they call such places in Filadelfia. He lounged in and bought it with a flurry of scholastic enterprise; his eyes and fingers had hungered for it. Having recently become secretary to the Curator of Antique Visual Arts at the Filadelfia Museum, Patric was making an earnest effort to develop a blind of scientific and aesthetic perceptions. He was always after developing something—memory, muscles, sexual staying power, executive ability—a splendid trait in young people, especially young secretaries.

Patric was twenty-three, born in 612. That was the year of the Trenton Convention when Penn, allied with Conicut, Nuin, and the other northern countries, took over the doddering Katskil Empire and established the Eastern Federation for all time or anyhow quite a while. It was the decade when the refinement of sailing ships made possible regular trade and communication with Europe and other far places, and we began to hear talk of a world federation and other marvelous dreams. Patric was a child of his age and would have said so himself. He enjoyed the coincidence that his life had started with the Convention that really did seem to have secured a lasting peace.

The image had a look of enormous age. To Patric's eye it was far out of harmony with his apartment's spanking new Seventh Century decor. The two faces, blackened and lithified by fire—maybe its smoke had dissolved into the sky when mammoths were roving the grasslands?—viewed time and change with a tolerance that reduced anything so brief as a century to a flurry and a squeak. Patric had first removed everything from the mantel except the image. But then the two-faced god reduced the entire living room to modern banality. His nice brass-and-glass whale-oil lamp became flashy and meretricious, the pewter candlesticks ginger-bready. His wool rug, an import from Main—too new, though it faithfully followed a patchwork pattern from the nineteenth century of the Christian period. And the scrolled woodwork, and—(O God, and O misery that he had to rent the damned place furnished!)—the plaster cherubs, the bug-gerly great frieze of plaster cherubs all around the room with fig leaves clinging to their theoretical rods and grooves by the power of faith alone! For you can't have everything, and our seventh century was after all an age that would give no offense even to that dear good lady of the faraway nineteenth, who was, among other things, Empress of India, and whose name for the moment escapes me. And the embroidered Holy Murcan texts framed under glass and glued to the wall in the sanitary modern manner so that viruses and drafts and unfavorable auras can't collect behind them. The late hus-band of the landlady Mam Gebler had paid 300 Penn dollars, pre-Convention value, inciting a journeyman artist to commit those cherubs. As for the texts, Mam Gebler's Aunt Essie—Esmeralda, the one who died of a kidney stone as big as your fist—had Done Them Herself.

There was no place for the image in Pat's bedroom except the bureau top. Primordial deities don't get on well with comb, brush, loose coins, bachelor socks. Aunt Essie had done another text especially for that room, by the way, the year Mr. Gebler died leaving hell's own pile of furniture and a passel of debts, which moved Mam Gebler to let out the place in furnished apartments for gentlemen with references. This text declared: THOU GOD SEEIST ME. Aunt Essie might have fucked up the spelling, but her anaphrodisiac intent was plain. She must have planned it as a defense for

138

Mam Gebler's chambermaids. It wouldn't have stopped Patric, who had invented sex seven or eight years earlier, but Mam Gebler never hired any chambermaid who wasn't ugly as dammit and meaner than a bobcat. Patric, by his own admission, was a lover of beauty and an admirer of kindness.

He quit trying to fit the image to the apartment, and began carrying it in the pockets of shirt or loincloth. Sometimes when he undressed it clonked on the floor. The image took no harm from that, being tough as granite from fire and the ages.

It stood no taller than a big chessman and weighed five ounces. Surely the maker's tools had been his fingers. The sex parts of both male and female sides were sketched in rude bas-relief against the blob of shared trunk and fused thigh-region, and the gouges told endearingly of fingernail work. It did not quite suggest a fertility image to Patric's scientific eye. In his reading Patric could find no reference to a true hermaphroditic god of antiquity. On both sides the arms were folded above the navel, dim marks indicating hands. Allowing for two sets of elbows, the artist had sculptured the forearms about half natural length. The blunt thigh-region ended flattened so the image could stand upright. The bottom was irregular as though someone had pressed the wet clay against a flat surface without trimming it.

Patric showed it one day to his venerated employer, the Curator Dr. (Sir) Winfield Hamlin, who placed it in the paper-leaved jungle of his desk and cleared his throat in long rattling blasts, mainly a device for keeping Patric's mouth shut while he reflected. "Ah, yes, there was a fad for things resembling this, fifty-odd years ago—time of the Republic— you know? Sixth century catchpenny trash. A lot of it originated here in Penn, naturally. But Yankee ingenuity also intervened—hrrr. A Boston style—yes—or was it Cambridge—bushwa-type art with a learned flavor for the tourist trade."

"Yes, I know, Sir Winfield—an expression of Harvard indifference perhaps. However, I didn't think this—"

"Of course not. Obviously old. Genuine. Don't confuse me. Aaargh." Dr. Hamlin shoved long knotty fingers through his dense white-sprinkled hair and clenched his domineering brows. "Where in hell'd you find it, Jonz, mind if I ask?"

"Dever's Odd-Goods on Brod Street. Buried among the tourist stuff. . . . Could it be Old-Time, sir?"

"Hhrraaa."

"I mean of course, *early* Old-Time. That is—"

"Hr."

"Could it, Sir Winfield, antedate the Christian era?"

"How you do go on! It is primitive art," said Dr. Hamlin, whipsawed in the fantastic difficulties of thinking while young people talk. "Of course. Hwaargh (ptui). Of course it antedates the Christian period, the Greek, the Egyptian, Assyrian, Mohenjo-Daro, the whatever. Wha'd Dever want for it, mind if I ask?"

"A dollar."

"Ass. Dever, I mean." Ghastly upheavals and realignments took place in the ragged moccasin-leather of Dr. Hamlin's face, possibly the onset of a sneeze. His attenuated frame, six feet five when fully unwound, fidgeted in the hard small chair which the Museum felt to be suited to its executives and department heads because it kept them awake. The facial temblor resolved itself into a gaunt and demoralizing smile. "Jonz—or Patric if I may—this thing of course is of no value, but had you considered—rrr—donating it to the Museum? Quite possible some stray corner could be found."

Patric thought: *Why, the old son of a bitch!—so now I know; or do I?* He retrieved the clay image and rubbed it with his thumb, seeing Sir Winfield wince and look away. "I don't know, sir. I've grown sort of attached to it."

"Quite natural, my boy. One often does, to these worthless things. In the presence of prehistory and all that bullshit. You know, it's possible the Museum might undertake to underwrite some infinitesimal solatium, a *quid pro quo* as it were—hard to say."

Beginning to feel dizzy with a sense of power, Pat inquired with the bloody bluntness of youth: "How much?"

"Why, good God, my dear boy, I couldn't possibly—oh,

some trifle, some nominal sum for the record. Hwaargh! The trustees have board meetings about things like that. I, of course, would be the logical one to bring it up before the—uh—the board.''

"I see. Perhaps I ought to think it over."

"By all means," said Sir Winfield in a weak voice. "Thought is the power that raises man above the beasts, if that's where he is." As Patric was politely escaping, he recovered partially, and roared a suffering addendum: "Don't you go showing that thing to any of my honored colleagues! You know there isn't one of those sods that wouldn't steal you blind!"

"I wouldn't think of it, sir."

"The goddamn board might go to five bucks."

"I must certainly think it over."

"You do that."

Ordinarily Patric dropped a penny in the hat for the beggar at the corner of Brod and Duli, but heading homeward toward the plaster cherubs that evening, he forgot. A placard certified the beggar to be a war veteran blinded at the battle of Ramapo in 602. Bare ends of thigh-bone showed how a surgeon had lopped them in a race with gangrene. A broad patch covered his eyes. Stung by neglect, the beggar mumbled a tired curse or two, learning not much from the lazy noise of Patric's receding steps. Patric Jonz was thinking about time, prehistory, civilization, the multiple faces of love and truth, and—*How much MORE than five bucks is it worth?*

The June air hung heavy with the scent of roses. From yards facing south, protected against the occasional frosts of winter, Patric also caught the bacchanal sweetness of blooming orange trees. Late sunlight was blessing the old city—four and a half centuries old at least, thought to be standing only a few miles from the site of a submerged metropolitan center of Old Time, that perplexing slice of backward infinity called by the Holy Murcan Church the Pagan Era, by others the Late Christian Period. A few have called it the Golden

Age of Science, or just the Golden Age, and some with more justice call it the Age of Spoliation, since the earth ever since then has been poorer than a straw-fed mule.

By the old church on Mark Street Patric made his usual pause. The venerable building enjoyed a lawn and garden space inside a six-foot brick wall; the weathered yellow bricks and the wheel-and-spire tower of the church were now reflecting a beginning crimson of sundown. The church sheltered a chapter of the ancient order of Franklinites, an enclave of strict piety in an increasingly secular age, vowed to silence and notorious for good works.

The Curator's opinion ought to be sound. The little twinned god must be old beyond explaining or comprehending. Prodigiously older than the Holy Murcan Church, which as recently as the last century had enjoyed an undisputed vested interest in eternity.

Before the church rose one of those tall obsolete iron stakes. Why the devil, Patric wondered, did they preserve such objects, as though modern Murcanity saw nothing evil in them? He stepped into the bushes that the church considerately allowed to grow outside the brick wall. He supposed, loosening his loincloth, that you could ask the authorities about it, but you wouldn't win much light. Certainly not on the question: Does the Church imagine it might one day use the stake again in the traditional manner? It would be more profitable to ask the question of one of the Franklinites, since his vows permitted no answer but a grunt.

Comfortable once more, Patric considered the graffiti on the upper section of the wall. It amounted to a valued message center. Every few days a Franklinite would march out in bitter silence with a mop and bucket to clean away the notices, invitations, self-descriptions, diagrams, wishful fancies, etc., because of the fearful danger that they might be observed by the young (who often had put them there). Thus one could feel sure that any important communication found here wouldn't be more than three or four days old; the citizens felt a decent gratitude to the fathers for thus keeping the information up to date. Patric gave thoughtful attention to some words that looked fresh: *Ask for Thalia at Mam Sola's house. I found merit in her discourse.* The script was literate, the message not the usual tribute to a five-dollar prostitute; Thalia must have pleased someone of exacting taste. Patric sighed, mentally reviewing his wallet. Twelve bucks and small change, payday four days off. One must forgo either eating, or Thalia. At Mam Sola's, he had heard from rumor, there were drinks to buy and maybe other extras. One would live on peanuts and crackers the rest of the week.

He wandered on to a Mark Street bar named The Whitish Virgin. It was pleasantly lit by the slipper-shaped whale-oil lamps recently come into style. They do smoke worse than lamps with a glass chimney, but they have some charm, if the veiling is vented to carry off fumes. In this hostel they stood on firm shelves, high enough to escape being knocked over in a brawl. The straw and shavings were clean. A nicely painted nude above the bar was doubtless the virgin who gave the place its name. She stood elegantly beside a canopied bed, smiling at the observer like a lemon cream puff.

Patric ordered a beer. The place was quiet at this early hour. Only one other drinker stood at the bar, a slender but muscular young man whose blue shirt carried the hammer insignia of the Construction Workers Guild. He glanced at the black pen design on Patric's shirt without awe. Members of the Clerical Guild had become almost common in the last thirty years, since the Church had been obliged to eff off with its restrictions on reading and writing. The blue-shirt said pleasantly: "Hot, a'n't it?"

"Ayah," said Patric, and smiled, nodding at the hammer insignia. "What branch?"

"Carpenter. As for the heat I figured you'd say that, but you people up here don't know what heat is. I've been down to the colony the last six months. Belltown, that's the asshole of creation. They needed carpenters and the pay was good. Twenty-six miles south of the Pottymack as the trail runs. Last settlement this side of Misipa, and the worst."

"There's been talk in the journals, government may decide to extend the colony all the way to the Misipan Wall."

"Been a lot of shit too. Meaning no disrespect to the journals—I know you Clericals go big for 'em."

"Not too big."

"Well, I call it stupid talk, about extending the colony. We're better off with a jungle no-man's-land between us and Misipa. Damned slaveholders. They built the wall, let 'em sweat behind it."

"Ayah. There's been mention of scouting parties in the jungle."

"Bullshit parties. I went on one of those. The jungle beyond the Pottymack is no place for human beings, Mister——never will be. What we did, see, we went off a little way into the big bush, far enough off so that Belltown folks couldn't see our campfire smoke, and set there with a thumb up. One of the boys had a gittur, and I play the corder, so the time passed nice enough. Then when we figured it was about right, our Clerical wrote up a report saying with a lot of big words that we hadn't found nothing, and so back to Belltown. By me it was a holiday, but not a real nice one, because that jungle is hell even if you ain't trying to travel."

"Ayah?"

"Believe me. Brown tiger's terrible, for one thing. There was at least two hanging around Belltown, and nobody could wing them—we had some damn good archers too. Lost three men. One was Bill Shawn, a friend of mine. The thing jumped a party he was with and carried him off in the broad day like a cat with a sparrow. You ever seen brown tiger?"

"Nay, never been out of Fil. I work at the Museum."

"That so? My name's Chad Snow."

"Patric Jonz."

" 'Know ya. . . . And the heat down there, man, and the wet, and the lonesomeness. Your moccasins look all right when you take 'em off to go to bed, come morning they're all over green mold. Scorpions. Centipedes eight inches long—the sons of bitches rattle when they run. You get tired from an amount of work that wouldn't even get you winded up here. And that ain't all."

"Sounds like enough."

"There are—well, Mr. Jonz, they call you crazy for believing them stories—I don't know—"

"Call me Patric."

" 'Kay—Patric. Stories about—small people, in the jungle. Little bastards, less than four feet tall. Three feet some say. Supposed to be descended from Misipan mues that were bred for slaves for several generations, and then revolted and took to the jungle. I don't *believe* it, but down there, if you get a touch of swamp fever or something, you start seeing things. You know—something just gone out of sight behind a tree bole. I ain't going back."

"Bartender—couple more beers, on me."

"Why, thank you kindly, Patric. It's great to be home."

Behind him Patric heard a minatory roar of throat-clearing. "Home," said Sir Winfield, "has been defined as a man's castle, where he can get away from everybody but himself. It's overrated. I myself was married once. Rraaargh. Through no fault of her own, the poor wretch could not abide me. She now runs a genteel seminary for young ladies of the upper social strata, God rest her, at Rasbury Park. Beer, bartender. I have a surpassing thirst."

Patric felt haunted. Would the Curator have demeaned himself by pursuing his secretary through the streets on some disingenuous errand? The thought was unworthy. However, Patric, maybe because of a spotless conscience, was not in the habit of looking behind him, so it could have happened. This was surely not Dr. Hamlin's preferred sort of bar. With his baronetcy and his income, he ought to favor high-toned drinking havens like the Penn Fathers Society, or the Art and Letters Club in the lush calm of Bethlum Street.

"Join us, sir," said Chad to the long old man who had already done so. "We were talking about the colony."

Patric mumbled introductions, hoping Chad would not be overimpressed by the "sir." He wasn't.

"Ah, the colony. An irrelevant political doodah superimposed on a contemptible patch of tropic efflorescence that would have been better left to the indigenous reptiles."

"I dunno," said Chad. "We done quite a bit of work."

"The Federation, in my view, would be better advised to further the liberal arts and allow the desuetudinous hinterland to remain *in statu quo.*"

145

"You may have a point there," said Chad.

"As an arcanum of indifferent hispidulate boscage, it might have its merits. Not that I wish to grind my own double ax, but the matter is self-evident."

"See what you mean," said Patric.

"Ain't he a corker?" said Chad.

"I am. By the term double ax I mean that the history of art must employ procedures of both art and science; thus I stand frequently before the imminent prospect of falling between two schools."

"Sir—"

"Later, Patric. I loathe being interrupted." Apologetically, he tapped Patric's arm. "The boy's my secretary, Mr. Snow, and besides, age has its privileges. Excellent beer. The fluid they describe as beer at the Penn Fathers Society is, beside this, diluted turtle piss. Your health, gentlemen!"

"How."

"Pros't," said Patric.

"The history of art, Mr. Snow, is my profession—that's why I drag it in by the ears."

"Call me Chad."

"With pleasure, Chad. And art is a wide subject. We must include, I suppose, the odorous mystique of politics, but we compensate for that by including the arts of brewing and distillation—ha! And of course the arts of love. Gentlemen, I give you love."

"Love," said Patric.

"Huh? Oh—sure. Love." Chad drank. "Ain't he a corker?"

"Yes. I am, it is true, a corker. Let me explain that. Before passing by here and most fortunately chancing to see you, Patric (if I may) I had already paused briefly at another oasis. There, at my very moment of entrance, a cork popped. Without human intervention. Spontaneously, I say, like the flight of a little bird. Rr."

Patric's fingers roaming in a pocket encountered the clay image, and he set it on the bar. The beer in the bottle of his brain had become an essential juice of benevolence. If he were to move his head it would slosh with love for all mankind. He did move it and it did slosh. "Let us drink to old gods and new loves."

"Admirable," said Dr. Hamlin.

Chad said: "Two arses, two faces, I be a son of a bitch."

Dr. Hamlin murmured: "And fingernail marks." A frayed gandyshank silenus, he lounged with intently brooding eyes, as though the sight of the image had swept him clear into the cool country of sobriety. "One may suppose he had no other tool at hand."

Patric suggested: "Maybe he (if it was he and not she) knew of no other tool?"

The Curator shook his head, in thought and wonderment, not in denial. Chad shook his head too, but nervously, as if at a buzzing fly. "I'd call that carrying marriage too far."

"You have a point there," said Patric. "Except I don't believe the artist was thinking about marriage."

"You mean he. . . ."

"Don't know. M' own philosophy marriage's very simple. Women. You got to treat 'em right. Love."

Sir Winfield said: "Patric (if I may) you are drunk."

"Nothing of the kind, sir. Slight nebriated is all. *In vino* lots of *veritas*. That's a fact."

"If he was sober," said Chad, "he'd know you got to treat 'em tough. Only way."

"No no," said Patric. "No, I deny that paregorically. Toughness is a weariness to the spirit, like for instance once upon a time said Adam to Eve, 'For God's sake! My back is one big solid ache. It ain't that I mind begetting mankind, but couldn't we take a short break?' "

"He's drunk," said Chad. "You have to treat 'em tough, rough."

"Tender."

"Gentlemen, gentlemen!"

Chad asked uneasily: "Who's the old corker talking to, Patric? You got any idea?"

Dr. Hamlin scratched his neck. "Gentlemen, I feel that your difference of outlook has been expressed in simple and basic terms upon which I cannot improve. Tenderness versus toughness. Rr. It raises a number of shrewd and difficult points; but I would suggest to you that we do, inevitably, approach the proposition solely, and it may be narrowly, from the masculine point of view. Now there is—"

"He's such a nice little guy," said Chad. "I hate to think of him being, you know, swallered up in the clutches of some—some—"

"I assure you," said Patric, "I have always been able to preserve the 'tegrity of a disintellected interest."

"Especially when he's drunk, like now."

The Curator inquired: "Do you boys want to be alone?" Chad didn't laugh. "I was about to say, there is a remedy for a too exclusively male presentment of our problem, namely the submission of it, accompanied I presume by demonstrations, to a qualified and impartial umpire—but first let me hasten to say that for the independent intelligence of both you gentlemen I have only the highest, the very warmest regard—"

"To you, sir."

"To you, Sir Winfield. Pros't."

"Thank you both, heartily. Now I should respectfully urge that in order to be qualified as a judge of the matter hereinbeforementioned, the umpire must be, as it were, a woman."

"Hear, hear!" said Patric.

"That statue," said Chad. "It kind of gets you."

"Thought you didn't like it," Patric said.

"Didn't at first. You have to get used to it. It gets you."

"An umpire capable by physical nature, namely a woman—"

"I mean it—*gets* you. Mind if I pick it up?"

"Not a bit. Go ahead."

"Balls," said Sir Winfield.

"No, honest, I was listening," said Patric. "And Chad here didn't mean to interrupt. You were talking about women."

"Well, I was merely trying to direct your thought and that of Mr. Snow to the consideration of a logical outcome, namely the reference of your basic conflict to a judicially minded member of that profession which for some odd reason is referred to as the oldest. (Actually I believe the skilled design and production of spiked clubs for bashing in the heads of neighbors is a far older profession than prostitution, but for the moment we will let that pass.)''

''What conflict?''

''Tenderness versus toughness. Alcohol seems not to improve the quality of your attentiveness.''

''Oh, that.'' Struck by a poignant certainty that one day Chad and he would be old weary men, the Curator dead, and that delightful wench—what was her name?—Thalia— Thalia might no longer have merit in her discourse, Patric felt darkly inclined to weep; manfully, he did not. ''Dare say Chad's pro'ly right.''

''What! Don't you stand up for your own views, young man?''

''Oh, I do, by *God* I do!'' Patric struck the bar, accurately, and ordered beer. ''Nothing counts with a woman like—like what did I say? Ten'erness. And of course staying power. I do not refer to quantity, a coarse conception. I would not have you think me on a level with Ezekiel Budworthy Gower, who could comfort six quail in one hour with nine minutes for each plus a very short speech explaining his curious power. But it's ten'erness that counts.''

''Would you bet on it, kid?'' Through the haze, Chad looked incoherently annoyed, though maybe not at him.

''Wouldn't be fair,'' said Patric. ''Here I am, known as a grandmaster of the erotic art throughout the civilized world—''

''Make it Filadelfia,'' said Dr. Hamlin.

''Known throughout Filadelfia as a lover without a peer. When I enter a room, women—you understand I'm zaggerating to make my point, but the principle is sound—when I enter a room—shit, Sir Winfield, what happens when I enter a room?''

''I don't know. But you are, in fact, willing to lay a wager on your position? I thought Mr. Snow's offer was eminently fair.''

"What offer?"

"Why, if I properly understood the drift of our discourse, it was proposed that we should attend an establishment of the better sort, and there submit your difference of opinion to the judgment of some judicially inclined hetaera, if such can be found. Mr. Snow then offered to place the matter in the form of a wager. I myself, as a neutral party, am prepared to hold the stakes."

"Got no stakes," said Patric. "Pay-day problem."

"Possibly," Dr. Hamlin murmured, "some material object other than coin of the realm. . . . As for the tariff at the establishment I mentioned, I am prepared to underwrite it in the interest of science and philosophy."

Chad burped and laid his knife belt on the bar. He pulled a ten-inch blade from a leather sheath and turned it so that the cold blue spat splendor in the lamplight. "Katskil steel that is. Look at the ivy design along the shaft."

"Remarkable," said Dr. Hamlin.

"Antique, too. Man that sold it to me said it was a hundred years old. Good as new, though. Wouldn't want to get in front of it. I've had it five years. If you're agreeable, Patric, I'll put it up against that cockeyed statue thing."

While Dr. Hamlin examined the old knife, Patric suffered a panic that he hoped would prove temporary. After all, his factual experience as a great lover was limited to an episode about a year ago with a doe-eyed waitress named Vickie who amused herself with him for a couple of months before very sensibly marrying somebody else. "Patric," she had said, "you are a sweet kid but you've got no sense. And no prospects." Well, what the hell—hope for the best. He mumbled: "Statue markable arche-o-logical significance."

"What?" said Chad.

"Oh, nothing."

"It's a deal?"

"Sure."

"Well, if the Professor's going to pay for the girls—"

"Girl," said Sir Winfield. "One of judicial mind. To assess the relative merits of the tough versus the tender approach—as if she didn't already know."

150

"All right. If the Professor's going to pay for the girl, le' me buy us a supper. Lead for the pencil."

"I will trail along," said Patric sadly, "in my capacity as a specter of gaunt poverty, useful walking comment on the depravity of the Lucullan table, and worth feeding if only for that reason."

"Oh, come on!" said Chad.

"I take this very kindly," said Dr. Hamlin, "although in exalting me to the academic height you do me a most undeserved honor, since I have never professed anything, except astonishment at the perpetual and quasiseraphic fatuity of humankind."

During supper at a nearby beanery Patric remained somewhat sad, although ready to admit, and prove, that the dust of the highway of life can at times be laid by beer. Chad tucked into roast mutton, mashed potatoes and apple pie, and said virtually nothing. Sir Winfield, gone into a genial twilight mood, discoursed knowledgeably on a literary phenomenon of the late Christian period which had gone by the curious name of science fiction. It amazed him, he said, that when the possible was already fantastic—when these hysterical earth-destroying multitudes were already surrounded by automotive vehicles, flying machines, ships capable of journeying under water with the instruments for planetary destruction in their holds, even elementary space-flight as far as the moon—they should still have found it necessary to strain after the impossible and irrational in pseudoscientific fairy tales. But it may have been (said Sir Winfield) a logical sort of compensation for disappointment and boredom, for the fact that in the field of genuine scientific discovery the sense of wonder had for them a very short life: Today's miracle was tomorrow's old sock. Consider for example the late Christian miracle called teevy, or sometimes telly. There really was such an electronic device, so long as the raw materials and technology had existed to maintain it—a box with a bulging illuminated front, like a pregnant soap dish, before which people sat in extended narcosis while images were transmitted from a central control point directing them to what they were expected to consume the following day. As sugar for the pill, the instrument also provided wholesome entertainment—soothing head-smashing, eye-gouging, shooting, disemboweling, all in vivid attractive color. An astounding feature of this device was that the subjects actually paid for the privilege of being thus mentally and emotionally back scuttled. Well, said Dr. Hamlin, to every age its own dementia, and our own will doubtless appear laughable to the inconsiderate people of the eighth or ninth century, ho-hum. "Um," said Chad.

The streets had become cool in the lamplit dark. "The place I have in mind," said Sir Winfield, "is known as Mam Sola's. It is, in my experience, a house of notable gentility, often catering to what I may term the academic trade."

"Right on, Professor!" said Chad, and Patric was moved to sing a popular item of the day, "Diddle Me, Dumpling, Di-doo-dah," in a careful baritone, while in view of the gay and almost impudicitous overtones of this charming lyric, Sir Winfield thought best to add, as a qualifying counterpoint, a rendition in A-major of "Rock of Ages," the two being somewhat blended by a strong patient monotone from Chad Snow in the general neighborhood of a low G-natural. Standing before another wall, imperfectly located but much needed, Patric said: "It seems to me we did that with distinction."

"Your A," said Dr. Hamlin, "in what I believe to have been the last chord, was abominably flat."

"Excuse me, sir: the original intention was to perform in A-flat."

"I regret, of course, the disparity in our views."

"I felt all right," said Chad.

"Ah, well! Ah, youth! I hope that you young gentlemen feel no slackening of ambition at this jitical cruncture. That is Mam Sola's house. The one with the rosy curtains. Down 'ere."

Chad said: "Y'hoo!"

"Rr—Chad o' man—I meant to speak of this earlier. When we present ourselves at Mam Sola's establishment we must restrain any (very natural) tendency toward abrupt sound patterns on the order of *Y'hoo!* It is not, sir, that one in any sense deplores the quality or the substance of—uh—*Y'hoo!* Purely a matter of doing the Romans.''

"Understand perf'ly," said Chad, and he laid a protective arm over the Curator's shoulders, reaching up without difficulty. "Don't worry single thing. *I* don't hold it against you, Professor, that you can't hold your likker. Nothing against *any* man can't holslikker. We're going to take care of you. Relax, Professor."

"If you truly feel this unsolicited academic advancement—"

"Right, Professor! Advance! Up and at 'em! Oopsadaisy!"

A cragfaced maid in black and white admitted them with a somber nod of recognition for Sir Winfield. Sober except in the legs, the old man asked after her brother, a policeman in the Tenth Ward.

"Well as could be expected, Sir Winfield. A'n't had no falling fits all week, and they're taking him off swamproot. Just so he don't overdo, the doctor says. If you'll wait in the parlor—?"

"Certainly. Is Mam Sola at home to guests? We have something to discuss that may interest her."

"To you, Sir Winfield, and any friends of yours, I am sure she will be at home. Will I request the presence of the young ladies?"

"Not yet, Hilaria. First we'd like Mam Sola's advice on a matter of substantial philosophical interest."

"I hope, Sir Winfield, it don't have nothing to do with them weekly inspections. Get her down, they do. We try, Sir Winfield. Nobody can say it against us that we don't try, Sir Winfield."

"I'm sure. No, this is just a matter of philosophy."

"Well, if that's all. I will inquire, sir."

Patric submitted to a squashy maternal armchair, perfumed and forgiving. He saw Chad's lips form and suppress a respectful *"Y'h—"* evidently heartfelt. Across the room from Patric hung a few severely drawn and quartered land-

153

scapes (but no wall mottoes) and a more advanced painting in the popular style called Modern Primitive, apparently dealing with the rape of Lucrece but in a manner that could give no offense.

From time to time a heavy red curtain at the far end of the room was bumpily but softly agitated, and parted an inch or so away from pleasant flesh that said "Ooh—parm me!" Chad leered at this evidence of intelligent life forms in extraparlorine space, Patric politely ignored it, and Dr. (Sir) Winfield Hamlin sighed.

Hilaria returned. "Mam Sola requests that you come upstairs to her private sitting room, being her arthritis is bothering her." Hilaria sniffed. "I will bring up the tea things."

"I know the way," said Sir Winfield, and he remarked to Patric and Chad with excusable vanity: "Constantia and I are old friends." He creaked up the stairway and ducked his head to ease his height through a doorway into a charming little sitting room done in gray and white with a dull red carpet and a pot of brisk geranium at the window. Mam Sola's rocking chair stood by a busy burdened sewing table. There were armchairs for guests, a tea table, and a few tasteful drawings, mostly of little cottages with here and there a well-conducted sheep. Mam Sola beamed.

"So delightful to see you again, Sir Winfield!" Without staggering, he stooped to shake hands with the delicate little soul. "Do excuse my not getting up—it's the arthritis. Ah, you and I are getting into the frosty I'm afraid, Sir Winfield, into the frosty. How fortunate that there is always the life of the mind!"

"Indeed yes, dear Constantia, and good works too—we mustn't forget good works." Sir Winfield made stately introductions.

The old lady smiled on Chad, and cocked her head at Patric with some curiosity. "Now I had a dear friend Lizette Jonz, librarian for thirty years at the Donner Street Church—a connection, I wonder?"

"I don't think so, Mam. My family was from Betlam."

"Ah yes, the Betlam branch. Lizette was very literary, you

know. Her poems were often published in the Murcan *Advocate*. There was one about the lilies of death and corruption that I always thought was particularly sweet—I must have a clipping of it somewhere. These are sad days, aren't they, Sir Winfield?'' Hilaria flatfooted in, loaded with tea things and gloom; Mam Sola poured, chatting on merrily. "But I often think of the past, especially the chariot races. Young people don't know what they've lost. Nothing but buggy and sulky nowadays—I know it's all progress and so forth, but it seems a pity. I always felt the chariot races at Lanster Field were so genteel!—you remember them, Sir Winfield. Teams used to come from as far as Jontown. All those splendid young men! And the Percherons! I used to take my girls over, you know, and the management always gave us a nice tent by the fairgrounds. Everything's changed now, nothing left but the bulgar element. Oh dear, I do so love my cup of tea in the evening! Now then, what's this Hilaria said you wanted to discuss? She said it was about theosophy, but I told her, I said, that can't be right.''

"Philosophy, dear Constantia.''

"I tell as is told to me,'' said Hilaria, and retired, hurt.

"It's odd,'' said Mam Sola. "This sweet little room often gives Hilaria one of her Moods. I feel we ought not to *yield* to such things, it being merely that the lady who previously owned this establishment passed away in this room at the age of seventy-two of a bilious attack. Spot of rum in your tea, Sir Winfield?''

"Thank you, my dear.''

"It was very peaceful I'm told, and so long ago too—not the least occasion for Hilaria to take on so about it. Now tell me about philosophy! I'm all of a perish to hear about it.''

Dr. Winfield told her, at his customary length or a little more, remarking in conclusion that a young lady named Thalia had impressed him on an earlier occasion as being well fitted for the rendering of a judicial opinion. This reached Patric through the semi-opaque glow of his love for humanity. Is it possible, he asked himself, that a Curator of Antique Visual Arts would write graffiti on a brick wall? The implications for the human future are astounding.

"But," said Mam Sola—and checked whatever she was about to say. Patric felt that a message passed between her and Sir Winfield; no doubt all was for the best. His head sloshed. "Hmm," said Mam Sola. "Judicial. Darling Thalia! We're all very fond of Thalia. So very *thoughtful* of you young genlemen to take an interest. And a wager!—dear me, how exciting. I always used to let my girls place little bets on the chariot races, you know—seemed to make it more interesting for them somehow, I can't think why. Thalia is a trifle more expensive, Sir Winfield. So well thought of, you know—I have been obliged to increase the honorarium to, ah, twelve dollars. Per hour or fraction thereof. That dreadful federal tax."

"We must pay for our political pleasures, Constantia."

"Mph! That's a ridiculous law that says they can't take it out in trade. Why, the bookkeeping it would save, if only a couple of my sturdier girls—"

"Constantia, my dear, the argument runs that tax money is a public trust, to be spent for what they humorously describe as the good of all. For this reason, as I understand it, the government insists on receiving it in a negotiable form for, and I quote, redeployment of basic resources. Now of course if some way could be found—"

"Oh, rootitoot, don't bother me with suchlike at my age!"

"But that would indeed," said Patric, "be a kettle of shoes of an altogether different color."

"You see?" said Chad. "You prob'ly thought he was asleep."

"So that will be twenty-four dollars plus tax," said Mam Sola. "Or—perhaps thirty-six, Sir Winfield?"

"Why, yes, thirty-six, my dear."

"So kind! Yes, just put it in the sewing basket. I'll go and speak to Thalia." The old lady paused in the doorway to chuckle at them, but she seemed faintly worried too. "Judicial—dear me! So very *original*, Sir Winfield!" She was gone for long minutes. Dr. Hamlin sat with his hands on the head of his cane and his chin on his hands, contemplating the young. Chad fidgeted. Patric sat quiet striving to encourage transcendental thought. Mam Sola rustled back into the room, and tapped Chad on the shoulder. ''Miss Thalia will be pleased to see this gentleman first. Second door down the hall.''

After Chad strode away, frowningly intent on his mission but looking rather less than tough, Mam Sola sighed and resumed her knitting, her neat small fingers busied with their share of the fabric of the world. The other ancient face, resting on folded hands, blinked slowly once or twice at Patric like the face of a mild old turtle in the sun. At some time, Patric unnoticing, Dr. Hamlin must have taken the stakes of the wager from his pockets and placed them on the tea table. Chad's antique knife lay there caught in the glow of Mam Sola's lamp, metal made living, a brightly savage phallic thrust. Beside it, the two-faced image was gazing directly and stolidly into Patric from its female side, as any girl might point out that eternity and so forth is all right if you want to bother with it, but—?

Patric understood after a while that the Curator was pronouncing his own doubtless illuminating commentary on these objects of art, but the old man's discourse was proceeding like an army of banners filing up a mountainside with no great hope of ever reaching a predicate verb, and Patric felt incompetent to give it adequate attention. It was still advancing, he thought, when his friend Chad Snow returned. Chad was not reeling exactly, only dazed and uncommunicative, sitting down, shaking his head with a bit of a snap, and saying: ''Man!''

From the shadowed doorway behind Chad—well, at that time too some soprano downstairs was singing delightfully to a mandolin—Patric felt himself to be observed by the large, placid eyes of a girl in a pink bathrobe—or dressing gown, or robe, or something—who considered him with calm bordering on unconcern, and pointed, with a smile and a stabbing motion of a delicate hand and outthrust forefinger—at Dr. (Sir) Winfield Hamlin. The Curator rose, bowed to Mam Sola, Chad, and Patric (in that order) and departed with Thalia.

To be chosen last is, by some lights, a mark of favor. It

may imply that one wishes to hold freshest the memory of the person last chosen. Maybe it may.

Patric would have liked to direct toward Chad one of those all-purpose inquiries on the order of "How are things?" or "Warm, ain't it?" or "How they hanging?" which are the pennies and nickels of conversation—they won't buy much, but they chink. Chad, however, had closed his eyes and rested his head on the back of his chair; Patric felt it kinder not to disturb him. Ten minutes later, though, Chad opened both eyes for the purpose of contemplating Patric and winking one of them.

Patric also winked. To the best of his ability he strove to make this wink convey sympathy, fellow feeling tempered by the lightest touch of intellectual superiority, and a reaffirmation of his—one should not say *belief* in the presence of so much muffled uncertainty—of his *hopeful trust* that when his turn with Thalia arrived he would have this wager snaffled, cornered, in the bag. A massive load for one wink to carry; too much. Chad went back to sleep.

Mam Sola knitted; now and then she hummed.

Dr. Hamlin returned, only a little short of breath. He peered down on Patric and performed a slight motion of the thumb.

The second door down the hall opened at Patric's knock— his mother after all had been a schoolteacher and early training in politeness leaves its mark. Thalia smiled and closed the door behind him.

She was neither tall nor short, but in between; neither blonde nor brunette, but in between; neither pretty nor homely, but—uh-huh. Patric said: "Well, hello! You know, I never know what to say?" Thalia smiled, and patted his arm with modest eloquence. She was neither young nor old.

Patric inquired: "Did they tell you about it?" Thalia looked puzzled. "I mean about the wager." Thalia nodded, and sat on the bed, patting the place beside her. The pink bathrobe slithered down around her hips; she was examining a pink-slippered foot and apparently finding it more important than the discussion, though without a hint of rudeness.

158

Patric sat by her. He hugged her tentatively. As she looked up at him, friendly but still-faced, he noticed that her gaze was centered on his mouth. Startled into what he immediately feared was an uncouth directness, Patric asked: "Darling, are you by any chance a deaf-mute?"

Thalia nodded. She made a motion or two with her fingers; Patric shook his head regretfully. On her bedside table lay a small slate and a piece of chalk. As she indicated them she shrugged, maybe a way of suggesting that the privilege of speech is overrated, or just saying that she didn't care about talking in this evanescent moment. Then she was caressing him, and he was responding, if not quite in the manner of a great lover, at least humanly. He was certainly being tender, he knew; it occurred to him also that maybe he wasn't being very exciting. Possibly that was why when she turned her face aside he suspected her of smothering a yawn.

She flung away the pink robe; his loincloth joined it. Laying back naked, she opened her arms imperatively, and Patric went into them, to lose himself in a quite satisfying little storm.

In the following quiet, forgetting her disability—if you can call it that in a world where everyone talks far too much and few ever mean what they say—Patric blurted: "Chad wasn't really tough, was he?" She had been looking toward his lips. She reached for the slate and wrote, *No, mostly he talked about you.*

Giving him no more than a glimpse of that, she rubbed out the words and wrote others: *To the Stakeholder: Let me think it over. I can't make up my mind.* She put the slate in Patric's hands and pointed amiably to the doorway. Impulsively Patric kissed her. She patted his rump kindly and gave him a little push.

Patric handed over the slate to the Curator, who viewed it lovingly and critically, slanting back his ancient head to bring the writing under his bifocals. He said: "Ah!"

"So exciting!" Mam Sola murmured. "My goodness, I nearly dropped a stitch, back there. What does she say?"

"Says she can't make up her mind."

Chad flung Patric an affectionate half punch. "Ain't she a corker?"

"Easily that," said Patric. "All of that."

"Ah—gentlemen. When a woman has one of these little dificulties about making up her mind, one of the vital factors, gentlemen, is *time*. Never, never rush these things! Would it therefore be agreeable to both of you if the valuable stakes of this wager were kept in a place of safety until such time as Miss Thalia finds herself enabled to reach a decision? I have in mind specifically the tastefully arranged, carefully catalogued, and efficiently guarded precincts of the Filadelfia Museum, Division of Antique Visual Arts."

Chad said: "Well, I be a—"

"Actually, gentlemen, I see no other way out of our difficulty that is not subject to justifiable criticism on either pratical or ethical grounds."

"Boys," said Mam Sola, "ain't he a corker?"

"How true that is, Constantia! Gentlemen, I await your views."

"Oh," said Patric, "I suppose she'll make up her mind some time."

Sir Winfield smiled with all his wrinkles. "My dear Patric (if I may) it occurs to me that she is under no such compulsion. Indeed I think I can say with some certainty that in this matter dear Miss Thalia will *never* make up her mind."

Chad asked: "Now, Professor, how can you be sure of that?"

"She promised me."

Barry N. Malzberg

MAKING THE
CONNECTIONS

I

I met a man today. He was one of the usual deteriorated types who roam the countryside, but then again I am in no position to judge deterioration; for all I know he was in excellent condition. "Beast!" he shrieked at me. "Monster! Parody of flesh! Being of my creation, have we prepared the earth to be inherited merely by the likes of you?" And so on. The usual fanatical garbage. More and more in my patrols and travels I meet men, although it is similarly true that my sensor devices are breaking down and many of these forms which I take to be men are merely hullucinative. Who is to say?

"I don't have to put up with this," I commented and demolished him with a heavy blow to the jaw, breaking him into pieces which sifted to the ground, filtered within. Flesh cracks easily.

Later I thought about the man and what I had done to him and whether it was right or wrong but in no constructive way whatsoever but there is no need to pursue this line of thought.

II

Central states that they recognize my problem and that

they will schedule me for an overhaul as soon as possible. A condition of breakdown is epidemic, however, and Central reminds me that I must await my turn. There are several hundred in even more desperate condition of repair than I am and I must be patient. Etc. A few more months and I will be treated; in the meantime Central suggests that I cut down my operating faculties to the minimum, try to stay out of the countryside and operate on low fuse. "You are not the only one," they remind me, "the world does not revolve around you. Unfortunately our creators stupidly arranged for many units to wear down at approximately the same time, confronting us with a crisis in maintenance and repair. However we will deal with this as efficiently and courageously as we have dealt with everything else, and in the meantime it is strongly advised that you perform only necessary tasks and remain otherwise at idle."

There is really little to be said about this. Protests are certainly hopeless. Central has a rather hysterical edge to its tone, but then again I must remember that my own slow breakdown may cause me only to see central and the remainder of the world in the same light, and therefore I must be patient and tolerant. Repairs will be arranged. While I await repair it is certainly good to remember that robots have no survival instinct built into them, individual survival instinct that is to say, and therefore I truly do not care whether I survive or collapse completely as long as Central goes on. Surely I believe this.

III

My job is to patrol the outer sectors of the plain range, seeking the remnants of humanity who are still known to inhabit these spaces, although not very comfortably. If I see such a remnant it is my assignment to destroy him immediately with high beam implements or force, depending upon individual judgment. No exceptions are to be made. My instructions on this point are quite clear. These straggling remains, these unfortunate creatures, pose no real threat to

Central—what could?—but Central has a genuine distrust and loathing of such types and also a strong sense of order. It is important that they be cleaned out.

In the early years of my patrol I saw no such remnants whatsoever and wondered occasionally whether or not Central's instructions were quite clear . . . maybe they did not exist . . . but recently I have been seeing many more. There was the man I killed yesterday, for instance, and the three I killed the day before that and the miserable huddled clan of twelve I dispatched the day before *that*, and all in all, in the last fifteen days, after having never seen a man in all my years of duty, I have now had the regrettable but interesting task of killing one hundred and eight of them, fifty-three by hand and the remainder through beaming devices that seared their weak flesh abominably. I can smell them yet.

I have had cause to wonder whether or not all these men or at least some proportion of them are hallucinative, figments of my unconsciousness, due to my increasing breakdown. I have been granted by Central (as have all of us) free will and much imagination, and certainly these thoughts would occur to any thinking being. There seem to be too many men after a period of there having been too little. Also, indiscriminate murder has disturbed me in a way which my programming had probably not provided; whether these remnants are real or not, I wonder about the "morality" of dispatching so many of them. What, after all, could these men do to Central? I know what they are supposed to have done in the dim and difficult past, but events which occurred before our own creation are merely rumor and I was activated by Central a long time after these alleged events.

Do we have the right to kill indiscriminately these men who, however brutalized, carry within themselves some aspect of our creators? I asked these questions of Central and the word came back. It was clear.

"Kill," Central said, "kill. Real or imagined, brutalized or elevated, benign or diseased, these remnants are your enemy and you must destroy them. Would you go against the intent of programming? Do you believe that you have the capacity to make judgments; you whose own damage and wear are so evident that you have been pleading like a fleshly thing for support and assistance? Until you can no longer activate yourself, you must kill.''

IV

It occurs to me that it would be a useful and gallant thing to build a replica of myself that would be able to carry on my own duties. Central's position is clear, my own ambivalence has been resolved . . . but my sensors continue to fail dramatically; I am half blind, am unable to coordinate even gross motions, can barely lift my beam to chest height, can hardly sustain the current to go out on patrol. Nevertheless, I accept the reasons why the patrol must continue. If these men represent even the faintest threat to Central who will someday repair me, they must be exterminated.

Accordingly, I comport myself to the repair quarters which are at the base of the tunneled circuits in which I rest and there, finding an agglomeration of spare parts, go about the difficult business of constructing a functioning android. I am not interested now in creating free will and thought, of course—this is Central's job anyway; it would be far beyond my meager abilities—but merely something with wheels and motor functions, dim, gross sensors that will pick up forms against the landscape and destroy them. Although I am quite weak and at best would not be constructed for such delicate manipulations, it is surprisingly easy to trace out the circuitry simply by duplicating my own patterns, and in less time than I would have predicted, a gross shell of a robot lays on the floor before me, needing only the final latch of activation.

At this point and for the first time, I am overcome by a certain feeling of reluctance. It certainly seems audacious for me to have constructed a crude replica of myself, a slash of arrogance and self-indulgence which does not befit a robot of my relatively humble position. Atavistic fears assault me like little clutches of ash in the darkness: the construction of forms, after all, is the business of Central and in appropriating this duty to myself, have I not in a sense blasphemed against that great agency?

But the reluctance is overcome. I realize that what I am doing is done more for Central than against it; I am increasingly incapable of carrying out my duties and for Central's sake must do everything within my power to continue. Soon Central will repair me and then I will dispose of this crude replica and assume the role which has been ordained for me, but in the meantime, and in view of the great and increasing difficulties which Central faces, I can do no less than be ingenious and try to assist it in my own way. This quickly banishes my doubt and I activate the robot. It lies on the floor glowing slightly in the untubed wiring, regarding me with an expression which, frankly, is both stupid and hostile. Clumsy, hasty work of course but cosmetics are merely a state of mind.

"Kill men," I instruct the replica, handing over my beam to it. "They live in packs and in solitude in the open places, they skulk through the plains, they pose a great menace to our beloved Central which, as we know, is now involved in repairing us all, reconstituting our mission. Destroy them. Anything moving in the outer perimeters is to be destroyed at once by force or by high beam," and then, quite exhausted from my efforts, to say nothing of the rather frightening effect which the replica has had upon me, I turn away from it. Cued to a single program, it lumbers quickly away, seeking higher places, bent on assuming my duties.

It is comforting to know that my responsibilities will not be shirked and that by making my own adjustments I have saved Central a certain degree of trouble, but the efforts have really racked me; I try to deactivate but find instead that I am racked by hallucinations for a long period, hallucinations in which the men like beasts fall upon my stupid replica and eviscerate him, the poor beast's circuitry being too clumsy and hastily assembled to allow him to raise quickly the saving beam. It is highly unpleasant and it is all that I can do not to share my distress with Central. Some ancient cunning, however, prevents me from so doing; I suspect that if Central knew the

165

extent of my ingenious manuevers—even though they were done for Central's sake—it would be most displeased.

V

My replica works out successfully and through the next several shift periods goes out to the empty spaces and returns with tales of having slain several hundred or thousand men. We have worked out a crude communications system, largely in signals and in coded nods and it is clear that my replica has performed enormous tasks out there, tasks certainly beyond my own limited means. I have created a true killing machine. My impressions of a vast increase in the number of men out there were not hallucinative or indicative of deteroriation at all but appear to have resulted from real changes in the conditions out there. These remnants seem to be reproducing themselves; also they are becoming bolder.

"Kill," I say to my replica every shift period before sending it out again. "Kill men. Kill the beasts. Kill the aggressors." It is a simple program and must be constantly reinforced. Also, tubes and wiring, because of the crudeness of my original hasty construction, keep on falling out now and have to be packed in again as the program is reconstituted.

Still and truly, my replica seems to need little encouragement. "Yes," it says in its simple and stumbling way, "yes and yes. Kill men. Kill beasts. Kill and kill," and goes staggering and into the empty spaces, returning much later with its stark tales of blood. "Killing. Much killing and men," it says before collapsing to ground, its wires and tubing once again ruptured.

I do what I can to reconstitute. My own powers are ebbing; there are times during which I doubt even the simple continuing capacity to maintain my replica. Nevertheless, some stark courage, a simple sense of obligation keep me going. The men out there in the empty spaces are breeding, multiplying, becoming strong, adding to their number by the hundreds; were it not for my replica, who has the sole

166

responsibility for patrol of this terrain, they might overwhelm this sector, might, for all I know, overwhelm Central itself. My replica and myself, only we are between Central and its destruction; it surely is a terrible and wonderful obligation and I find within myself thus the power to go on, although I do admit that it is progressively difficult, and I wonder if my replica, being created of my own hand, has not fallen prey to some of my own deterioration and may, through weak and failing sensors, imagine there to be many more men than there actually are.

Nevertheless, and at all costs, I go on. I maintain the replica. Somehow I keep it going, and toward the end of the first long series of shift periods, I have the feeling that we have, however painfully, at least struck some kind of balance with the terrible threatening forces of the outside.

"Like kill men. For you," my replica says once which in my acid heart I find touching.

VI

I have not heard from Central for a long time, but then I receive a message through my sensors indicating that my time for repair has arrived, and if I present myself at the beginning of the next shift period I will be fully reconstituted. This news quite thrills me as well it should, although it is strangely abrupt, giving me little time to prepare myself for the journey toward repair, and Central is at a good distance from here, fully three levels with a bit of an overland journey through the dangerous sectors apparently populated by men.

Nevertheless, I present myself at the requested time, finding no interference overland. My replica has done an extraordinary job in cleaning out nests of the remnants, either that or my sensors by now are so entirely destroyed that I can perceive virtually nothing. In any event, I come into the great Chamber of Humility in which the living network of Central resides and present myself for repair. There is a flicker of light and then Central says, "You are done. You are completely repaired. You may go."

"This is impossible," I say, astonished but managing to keep my tone mild. "I am exactly the same as before. My perceptions falter, I can barely move after the efforts of the journey and I sense leakage."

"Nevertheless," Central says, "you are repaired. Please leave now. There are many hundreds behind you and my time is limited."

"I saw no one behind me," I say, which happens to be quite the truth; as a matter of fact, I have had no contact with other robots for a long period. Sudden insight blazes within me; surely I would have found this peculiar if I had not been overcome by my own problems. "No one is there," I say to Central, "no one whatsoever, and I feel that you have misled me about the basic conditions here."

"Nonsense," Central says. "That is ridiculous. Leave the Chamber of Humility at once now," and since there is nothing else to do and since Central has indicated quite clearly that the interview is over, I turn and manage, somehow, to leave. My sensors are almost completely extinguished; I feel a total sense of disconnection; still, out of fear and respect for Central, I obey the bidding. Outside in the corridors, however, my network fails me completely and I collapse with a rather sodden sound to the earth beneath, where I lay there quite incapable of moving.

It is obvious that I have not been repaired and it is obvious that Central has broken down and it is obvious that my hapless journey for repair has completely destroyed the remains of my system, but nevertheless, as I lie there in black, my sensors utterly destroyed, I am able to probe within myself to find a sense of discovery and light because I have at least the comforting knowledge that my replica exists and will go on, prowling through the fields, carrying out the important tasks of survival.

VII

Lying there for quite a long time, I dream that I call upon my replica for assistance. "Kill me," I say, "kill me, put me out of my misery, I can go on no longer, save me the unpleasantness of time without sensation,'' and my replica, wise, compassionate, all stupidity purged (in the dream I can see him; sight has been restored), bends over me and with a single, ringing, merciful clout separates me from my history, sends me spinning out into the fields themselves where the men walk . . . and among them I walk, too, become in the dream as one of them, only my replica to know the difference when he comes, on the next shift period, to kill. To kill again. To save the machines from the men.

THE BRIGHTEST STARS IN BERKLEY'S GALAXY
THE ALPHA AND OMEGA OF SCIENCE FICTION

CONTINUUM 1   (N2828—95¢)
  ed. by Roger Elwood

CONTINUUM 2   (Z3127—$1.25)
  ed. by Roger Elwood

CONTINUUM 3   (N3022—95¢)
  ed. by Roger Elwood

GALACTIC POT-HEALER   (N2569—95¢)
  Philip K. Dick

THE MOUNTAINS OF THE SUN   (N2570—95¢)
  Christian Leourier

ORBIT 13   (N2698—95¢)
  ed. by Damon Knight

THE STARS MY DESTINATION   (Z2780—$1.25)
  Alfred Bester

NIGHTMARE BLUE   (N2819—95¢)
  Dozios & Effinger

PSTALEMATE   (N2962—95¢)
  Lester del Rey

Send for a *free* list of all our books in print

These books are available at your local bookstore, or send price indicated plus 25¢ per copy to cover mailing costs to Berkley Publishing Corporation, 200 Madison Avenue, New York, New York 10016.